Flight Into Reality

Also by Greta Manville

The Purgatory Trail
(with Cleo Lorette)

Murder Online
(written as G. C. Manville)

Death Key

Transitions
(editor of a collection of essays, short stories and poems)

Flight Into Reality

GRETA MANVILLE

iUniverse, Inc.
Bloomington

Flight Into Reality

iUniverse books may be ordered through booksellers or by contacting:

iUniverse
1663 Liberty Drive
Bloomington, IN 47403
www.iuniverse.com
1-800-Authors (1-800-288-4677)

ISBN: 978-1-4759-5703-7 (sc)
ISBN: 978-1-4759-5704-4 (e)

Library of Congress Control Number: 2012919736

Printed in the United States of America

iUniverse rev. date: 10/26/2012

For Cleo Lorette, friend, teacher

and guide through the perils of creating fiction

Chapter

ONE

GARRICK THOMAS EDGED CLOSER to the rim, looked over the cliff's edge to the crashing sea far below. One more step and he would sail from this tropical island asylum, suspended—free from all restraints until the outcrop of boulders broke his fall. He wondered what he would feel in those first moments of freedom.

Release?

Regret?

"Hello, my name is Irene."

Startled by the soft voice, Garrick lurched backward from the precipice to grab the iron rail. As he turned, he looked into the pert, upturned face of a tiny, seventyish woman.

"You must be more careful," she chided. "You might have fallen."

"Uh … yes." Caught mulling his demons, his yearning for oblivion, Garrick ducked under the railing, embarrassed. With an ungainly wobble, he reached to grip the seatback of an ornate stone bench set alongside the path. His knees buckled, and he landed hard on the bench. "Oof!"

After a moment to compose himself, he patted the seat. "Come, sit beside me, Irene. Tell me who you are while we share this magnificent view."

He looked into her tranquil blue-green eyes, eyes the exact shade of the sea stretching across the immense horizon.

The woman smiled and settled on the bench, leaving a modest space between them. "It is lovely here, isn't it? Simply lovely."

A yellow warbler watching from atop a nearby Cayman thatch palm tittered and fluttered away.

Garrick's eyes followed a flock of graceful black skimmers as they flew low over the lapping waves along the beach below, diving for small fish and insects. He took a deep breath, fought to shake his spirits free from the clinging depression that so weighed upon his thoughts, his soul. "Irene, you say?" He forced a smile. "Are you Irene, as in 'Goodnight, Irene'?"

"No, Irene as in Irene Dunne."

"Really?" He squinted for a closer look. "I guess you do resemble the actress somewhat."

"I don't have to *look* like someone I want to be. All I have to do is just *feel* like her, and today I feel like Irene Dunne when she starred in that wonderful film *The White Cliffs of Dover.*"

"We have the cliffs, certainly, though we're a bit off from Dover." He waved toward the edge of their rampart overlooking the Caribbean. "I guess you could call the cliffs white, whitish, anyway. Dover's cliffs lack the dense jungle growth at the bottom, however. We'll just ignore that little detail." He could play along, welcoming any amusement her fantasy offered. He felt better already.

"The cliffs don't have to *be* white," she said.

"You have a jolly good imagination at work, Irene. Are you new here? I don't recall running into you around our 'campus'." He nodded toward the crescent of resort-style white stucco buildings with red tile roofs, all lining the far side of a promenade dotted with tall coconut palms. Several small cottages beyond the green mall sat sandwiched between two-story apartment buildings, administrative offices and an infirmary. "Nor have I seen you in our one and only store, the so-called 'company store' where we're allowed to shop. With the help of nurse's aides, of course, to make sure we don't pilfer emery boards or other valuables."

She ignored the bitterness of his words. "I wasn't well when I first arrived, but I'm fine now." The woman tidied her skirt and crossed her ankles before patting a loose gray-blonde wisp of hair into place. "You sound British."

"I am."

"I'll bet your name then is Trevor."

"A good guess, but you're wrong. Try again."

"I thought all you Brits were Trevors. As in Howard."

"Trevor Howard, I see. You *are* into old movies, aren't you, Miss Dunne?"

"Some days, I'm Marlene." She pronounced it Mar-LAY-nuh.

"As in Dietrich?"

"Of course."

"That should be interesting." He gave a Groucho tap to his imaginary cigar and waggled his abundant white eyebrows. "Then Irene isn't your name after all?"

Her petite face turned up toward his and her eyes crinkled in a coquettish smile. "No, you'll have to guess it. Like you're making me guess yours."

"That's easily resolved. My name is—"

"No!" She stopped him with pressure on his arm. "No, don't tell me. If I don't know your name, I can continue the fiction. I can pretend you're anyone I want you to be."

"Aha! It's clear that you're another of the famous mystery authors boarding in one of our, ah, vacation villas."

"Hardly vacation, more like retreat—from life." The edge in her voice relayed the switch to bitterness he saw in her eyes.

"Don't be angry." His hand brushed her smooth cheek and returned the errant tendril to its proper place. He marveled at how few wrinkles lined her face and wondered at her age. She identified with film stars of the Thirties and Forties, but anyone could do that if they watched enough old movies on TV—or were old enough to have seen the first runs. "Your eyes match the brilliant color of the sea. You should have your portrait painted with the ocean behind you."

She murmured, almost under her breath, "That was done in another life."

"Oh?"

"When my husband was alive … before I became ill."

"And where is that painting now?"

"My daughter has it at her apartment in New York, Manhattan actually." Her voice lightened. "She—Lauren—is coming to visit."

"And I suppose that would be Lauren Bacall?"

With a silvery laugh, "Irene" answered, "No, her name really is Lauren. Lauren Hale."

"What a pretty name."

"She'll be here soon."

"Yes, they all say that."

"Lauren always keeps her word. She is a wonderful daughter. Do you have children?"

"A son and a daughter-in-law, one grandson and one on the way."

"Don't they come to visit?"

He shook his head. "Let's be realistic. Our families parked us here out of sight and out of mind." He grunted. "Though it's we who are out of mind, they contend."

She looked alarmed. "What do you mean?"

He held her eyes, then looked away. "Why are you here?"

"My daughter said I was sick for a long while. I guess I lost track of time. She said the doctor thought I needed to get out of the city's stale air. Before that, Lauren insisted I live with her, but my home is in Arizona."

"How did you end up here?"

"The doctor found this health spa with its therapists, so Lauren brought me to Encantadora. She said it would help me return to my writing amid the beauty and serenity of the island while mingling with other writers."

"When was that?"

She hesitated. "I don't remember exactly."

"You said you were ill."

"When I woke up, I was here, and I feel wonderful now."

"I'm glad." Her sweet calm voice soothed his soul. Garrick took her hand, but she quickly drew it away and glanced at her wristwatch.

"It's late. Mother is expecting me for dinner." Her voice became light, agitated. "I must hurry now. She'll be angry if I'm late."

"Your mother? Is she a pa—, a guest here too?"

"Oh, no."

"Then you mean the Mother Superior of a Catholic convent? I didn't know there was one on this tiny island."

"No! I mean my *mother*. She's been cooking and cleaning all day, and I must help. She's tired." She rose from the bench without another word and hurried off along the pathway.

His lightened mood sank as Garrick called after her, "I'll see you in my dreams, Irene." *If only I could.* His thoughts turned bleak again as a remnant of horror flickered through his mind, a relic from his afternoon nap.

With the woman out of sight, he climbed again under the guardrail to walk to the edge of the cliff. He looked down at the swirling white foam. It would be so easy to end the terror here. A mere step could destroy the fiends overrunning his nightmares when the evil characters from his horror novels metamorphosed into composites to bring new terror, leaving him afraid to close his eyes, afraid to sleep. He was weary to death of battling these nightly, now even daytime, phantasms far crueler than any he had ever committed to paper. Pandora's box seemed to burst open inside his brain, spewing out fragments of monsters he himself had created while reinventing themselves as his own personal, punishing demons. The worst was Phelan. Phelan Powell, the vilest, most loathsome creature man could have summoned up in his imagination. Neither alcohol nor drugs had removed the curse that landed him at this posh island clinic for the insane.

He climbed back to the safety of the pathway. *Maybe if I rename myself Trevor they won't find me.*

Chapter

TWO

RESTLESS, SLEEPLESS, GARRICK PACED across the soft carpet of his cottage in the midnight darkness. The only illumination came from the window facing the mall. Grateful to share the dwelling with no other, he fought now to clear cobwebs from his dream, relics clouding his mind, strangling his thoughts.

Once again, the deranged killer from his earliest best-seller, Phelan Powell, lurked deep within Garrick's soul, struggling to free himself. Garrick stopped before a mirror over the living room highboy, shocked to see Phelan's dark, shaggy beard rather than his own clean-shaven face, the hair unkempt, the eyes wild. Garrick stared, tried to force the image back to its lair where it dwelled deep inside his brain. Instead, he caught the reflection of two men grappling on the mall with what seemed murderous intensity. The light shining from the lamppost outside his window revealed the battlers for only seconds before they wrestled farther toward the center of the mall.

In shocked silence, Garrick pondered whether the figures were real or one more manifestation from his overwrought mind.

The face in the mirror now morphed into his own familiar visage. Garrick hurried to the window. Were those Phelan's hands clutching the throat of the smaller man who sank to his knees? Garrick threw open the window and yelled, "Stop! What are you doing?"

Phelan looked up. Even from that distance, Garrick could see Phelan's black eyes boring into his, setting his brain on fire. Garrick continued to yell until the monster ran away, leaving his victim lying on the ground, lifeless.

Garrick slammed the window shut and closed the blinds. Another dream, eyes wide open. He turned on the bathroom light to find and take a second pill to help him sleep. He poured a paper cup full of water, gulped down the pill, and turned off the light before crawling back into bed.

❋ ❋ ❋

Mara Edwards, no longer Irene, awoke at the sound of a man's shouts, the voice familiar, like that of the nice gentleman she'd spoken with … when? She couldn't quite remember, but it seemed like perhaps … recently.

She hurried to the open window of her second floor apartment facing the mall. Two men were fighting on the mall, and it didn't look like horseplay. The lamplight near the cottage next door revealed what appeared to be a deadly struggle between two men she didn't recognize. Or did she? Could one of the men be that handsome young fellow, Kyle Vinson, the new therapist? He wore the orange shirt and white shorts of all staff members, their uniforms. The loose clothing of the other man looked like pajamas. Why would a staff member abuse a guest of the resort at any hour, let alone the middle of the night? This didn't make sense—it frightened her.

The man in pajamas collapsed to the ground, and the other man ran off. The yelling stopped. Mara wondered if she should call the main office to report what she'd seen, but how could she be sure in the darkness outside? Maybe they were just drunk and acting silly.

Nevertheless, she picked up the phone, hesitated, set it down. She went back to the window in time to see the staffer return and drag the other man out of her sight, past a tall palm lining the walkway. What on earth was going on?

She nearly tripped, hurrying to the phone. Mara rang the office.

A sleepy voice answered, "Jerry here."

"I, um, saw something very awful out on the green. Two men were fighting, and one fell down. The other man dragged him away."

"Uh-huh. Where were you?"

"In my room, but I heard shouting and went to the window."

"You're sure it wasn't a dream?"

"No, no. I'm wide awake."

"Did the shouting wake you up?"

"Yes, but I wasn't sleeping very well."

"I see. We'll check into it, ma'am. You go on back to bed now, and I'll have someone talk with you about it tomorrow."

"You'll send someone out now to look for the injured man? I'm sure he needs help."

"Sure. We'll take care of it. Don't worry."

Mara couldn't go back to sleep after witnessing the horrid incident. The nurse had given her the usual nighttime pills, but with all this excitement, she felt jittery, wired up. At the window, she watched for a while to see if anyone came out to look for the men, to check the grounds. They surely couldn't miss the signs of a scuffle in the damp grass if they brought flashlights.

Minutes passed. No one arrived to investigate. Why not? Didn't the man believe her? She began to fidget. Unable to resist the temptation, after many years of creating best-selling mysteries and horror stories, she had to find out what had happened.

Mara donned her bathrobe and slippers, then crept down the back stairs to avoid the noise of the elevator, which might awaken other residents if they weren't wide awake already after all the racket. She knew the two-story building wasn't staffed with night attendants, or she could have called whoever was on duty, someone close enough to see and hear the noise from the mall. She sensed Jerry didn't believe her. The administrative building faced one end of the mall, a fair distance from her apartment, and overlooked the boat dock below on the far side. The building housed staff dormitories as well as the business offices. If she walked over there, maybe she could make Jerry, or someone, anyone, believe her.

The June night, silent but for the distant susurration of the ocean, was warm, humid and scented with the fragrance of frangipani. A full moon hung over the tree tops. She felt no fear as she stopped on the sidewalk between her building and the cottage next door while she scanned the mall. The moon's brightness cast enough light to explain why she had been able to see the men so clearly. She wondered at the hour. Why hadn't she checked the clock beside her bed? She walked gingerly to the spot where she thought the man had fallen, the grass beneath her slippers still damp from a late afternoon shower. The grass seemed packed down where the men had fought, but she couldn't see whether a path had been left from the dragging of the body.

Despite the warm night, she shivered. What business did she have out here in the middle of the night where bad things had happened? She started to turn back toward her apartment building when a door to the cottage beside her building opened. A man lurched toward where she stood on the green. She steeled herself for an assault.

"Oh! It's you. Trevor!"

The man stopped, looked confused. "Irene. What are you doing here?"

Irene? Who is Irene? "I'll ask you the same question."

"I saw fighting a bit earlier. Or I thought two men were fighting."

"Yes, so did I. Was it you who called to the men?"

"I shouted but thought I was having a nightmare and went back to bed. I still couldn't sleep and tossed about for a while. When I looked again, I saw you standing here in the moonlight. I didn't recognize you, but my curiosity was piqued, so I came out. What is your real name, by the way?"

"Mara. And you are …?"

"Garrick. I guess we can stop playing your little game."

Mara wasn't sure what he meant. She remembered talking with him, though not what they'd said. She remembered calling him Trevor, but who was this Irene? And maybe he was part of the brouhaha she'd witnessed, so maybe it wasn't a good idea to be standing here talking with a more-or-less stranger now. He'd admitted that it was his voice she'd heard shouting. "I'm going to my room. We can talk tomorrow."

"Wait. I'd like to know what you saw."

"And so would I." A tall Jamaican, Samuel, the sole security guard on the island, stepped from the shadows. "What are you two doing out here?"

"I told the night attendant, Jerry, that I saw two men fighting. Did he call you?"

"No. The only commotion I heard was you two."

"Jerry said my report would be checked out in the morning," Mara protested. "I don't think he believed me."

"Did you recognize the men?"

"One, maybe. Did you … Garrick?"

"I thought so, but sometimes I suffer from nightmares."

Mara hesitated to implicate anyone without confirmation from Garrick. He'd witnessed the fight, so why not admit it?

"Tell me what you saw." Samuel's baritone voice, with its pleasant island accent, was firm but not intimidating.

"I thought I saw that nice young man, Kyle," Mara said. "The new one. At least, I thought he was nice. I saw Kyle—that's his name—drag the man away. The man looked like he was dead."

"Dead or just unconscious?"

"He wasn't moving."

"What else did you see?"

"It was awful. First, the fighting, then the choking. The man kicked and screamed, before he went limp like a rag doll." She shuddered, acted out the limpness.

"And you?" The guard turned to Garrick. "What did you see?"

"I thought I saw two men fighting, but … I couldn't identify either man," Garrick said. "Mara told you she saw the injured man taken away."

"A terrible thing," Mara said. "The attacker wore an orange shirt and white shorts—like all of you staffers." She nodded toward Samuel in his identical attire. "I'm fairly sure Kyle was the one who dragged him away. I'm not too old to notice that Kyle has nice legs. I recognized his legs."

"Do either of you know the man?"

"I told you it was *Kyle*!" She could be firm, too.

"The *injured* man, I mean."

Garrick and Mara shook their heads, no.

"Maybe Kyle took him to the infirmary," Samuel suggested. "I will check over there."

"I'm not sure they went in that direction," Mara said, exasperated by everyone's slow reaction. "I couldn't see past that palm tree." She pointed to the tree that had blocked her line of sight.

"Don't you have electronic surveillance?" Garrick asked. "I'm surprised you didn't observe the activity."

The guard looked uncomfortable. "I was occupied. It will be on tape for me to review."

"There you go," Garrick said, "to hell with the poor bugger who might still be alive. I'm turning in. How about you, Mara?"

"I'm very weary."

As they started to leave the mall, Jerry, the night desk attendant, faced them. "What's going on?" he asked. "What are you two doing out here?"

"We're providing the security guard with information," Garrick answered, his voice gruff. "We're not dancing by the light of the moon, in case that's what you think we lunatics do."

Jerry turned to Mara. "I told you we'd investigate in the morning. I suggest you get some sleep." He shined the flashlight over the grass.

Mara wondered why he'd waited so long to look around. "If people were doing *their* jobs, we'd be asleep by now."

Garrick grunted, "Right on."

Samuel hurriedly told Jerry what little he knew.

Jerry pulled out his pager. "Kyle. Get over to the mall in front of building five. Stat!"

Kyle appeared within minutes, in orange T-shirt and white shorts, his thick dark hair rumpled. "What's this all about?"

Mara shrunk back against Garrick, then moved as quickly away.

Jerry explained the situation, disbelief evident in his voice. "She said you fought with someone then dragged the body off somewhere." Jerry again flashed light over the grassy area so recently trampled by the witnesses.

Kyle scratched his head. "You're kidding. What could she have seen in this darkness? I've been asleep for several hours. She must have had a bad dream."

Mara heard Jerry lower his voice and conclude, "Or OD'd on meds."

"You think we both had the same dream?" Garrick interrupted. "That a man was not beaten right here less than an hour ago? A man that we both saw?" An image of Phelan passed through his mind. "I'm not sure the man wasn't strangled."

"Are you sure it wasn't a couple of guys horsing around?" Kyle asked.

"In other words, we're nuts. Time to give us another pill."

Mara placed her hand on Garrick's arm in an attempt to calm him. "It seemed so real," she said, softly. "I'm afraid to go back to my room alone." Moreover, she felt uncomfortable in Kyle's presence after fingering him as the aggressor in the ugly affair.

"It's all right, Mara. You can stay with me," Garrick said. As much as he cherished his privacy, the poor woman needed companionship. And maybe so did he.

"I don't know ..." Jerry began.

"You don't know anything," Garrick finished. "I'll look after the lady—or she'll look after me." He put his arm around Mara's shoulders and led her toward his cottage.

"Kyle," Jerry said, "they could use something to calm them down. Have you got a key to the meds?"

"Sure." Kyle left for the office.

"I don't need anything," Garrick said.

"I do," Mara whispered.

"Only a mild sedative," Jerry explained. "It will help you go back to sleep after the fright. And don't worry, we'll thoroughly check into whoever is missing and what could have become of him."

"That's comforting," Garrick growled.

"I'd start with Kyle," Mara said. "I know what I saw."

Once inside Garrick's cottage, he closed the door and lowered himself to a club chair while Mara huddled at the end of his sofa. A tap on the door startled her.

"Come in," Garrick called, his voice gruff.

Kyle entered carrying two pill cups and small water bottles. He set them on the coffee table and uncapped the water.

Mara froze at the sight of the man, so near—and they were alone with him.

"I don't want one of those," Garrick said, pointing to the pills.

"I'm sorry, sir. I'm following orders."

"Whose orders, that little peanut vendor from the office? You don't have to answer to him."

"Orders in the chart, sir."

"Let me see that chart."

"I don't have it with me. The chart is written by the doctor who prescribes medication to calm residents who become distur—, upset for any reason."

Mara reached over for her pill cup and quickly took the water bottle from Kyle's hand. She gulped the pill and settled back. "Is it all right if I stay here with Garrick tonight? We'll behave, won't we Garrick?" she asked, with a nervous laugh, certain only that she didn't want to be alone.

Garrick grumped before swallowing his pill. "I might as well put my lights out, too." With a devilish nod toward Mara, he added, "If you're going to make me behave."

Kyle looked relieved and made a swift departure, job done.

"Wonder the man didn't try to drag our bodies off," Garrick muttered. "You may have my bed, dear, though it hasn't been changed this week."

"Oh, no, that's all right, Garrick. Just give me a blanket, and I'll be okay here with this pillow. Is the door locked?"

Garrick rose and turned the lock. "It is now." He took a lightweight blanket from a cupboard beside the door. "I say, I find this all very distressing."

"The man … it was so awful."

"Yes, the man. And the letter I received from my son, Geoffrey, Geoff, after our little visit today."

"Where does he live?" Mara yawned, stretched out, and pulled the blanket over her shoulders.

"In England, in our old country house. I haven't seen Geoff in five years—not since he dumped me here."

"You've been here five years?"

"I had a problem with alcohol. A lot of writers do, you know. Especially the great ones," he laughed. "Geoff sent me to dry out. Well, I've been … fairly dry for five years. At least, I have the problem under control. For a long time, I didn't want to leave. It's beautiful here, you know, and quiet most of the time, away from people, things."

"Yes, but it's beautiful in Arizona too, and I'd rather be in Arizona."

"On the whole, I'd rather be in Philadelphia." Garrick tapped an imaginary cigar as he mimicked W. C. Fields' suggestion for his epitaph.

"I don't know why I'm still here now that I'm well. There's nothing wrong with me." She yawned again. "I think Lauren will take me home, back to Arizona."

"At first, I had the energy to write. I have a computer." Garrick pointed toward his bedroom where a desk was visible through the doorway. "Geoff set me up with one, so I've used it, but I preferred my old portable typewriter. Now, I suppose I should familiarize myself with the internet, so I could get out of this friggin' hell hole, excuse me, at least mentally." He laughed. "I should e-mail the authorities: S. O. S."

"Will your son come soon to take you home?"

"No. His wife is pregnant—again—and won't fly after losing two prior pregnancies, so Geoff will stay to take care of her. They don't want me there. I was in the way."

"Oh, now, I doubt that. Maybe Lauren can help you go home too. She's very smart."

"I think you're imagining that your daughter is coming."

"No, I'm not!" Mara verged on tears. "She wouldn't lie." Her voice slurred, and her eyelids felt heavy. "Don't tell me things like that. I'm going to sleep now."

"You're right. Sleep well, old dear, and tomorrow we masterful creators of mysteries will solve the big one."

"Which is?"

"How to get out of here."

Garrick turned off the lamp and trudged toward his bedroom, muttering that he wished he had a cigarette. A cigarette and a drink.

"Good night," Mara called after him, her soft voice drowsy. She fell quickly asleep.

Chapter THREE

Mara awakened, chills gripping her shoulders, tingling her spine. In the gray dawn light, she recognized ... nothing. Who brought her to this unfamiliar place? Then she remembered the ragged, dirty man who tried to rape her. Burian. The evil man had followed her again, overpowered and dragged her here. But she had been clever and escaped to hide in a stranger's house.

Whose house is this? Is Burian still here somewhere? Did he—? Oh, no!

She jumped up from the sofa. Lifted her robe and nightgown. Investigated. No underwear. "Oh!"

Mara bolted for the door, fumbled with the lock and escaped, relieved to find tranquility with no one around, only birds coasting from tree to tree across the mall. Despite the early hour, not yet sunrise, the warm breeze took away her chills, soothed the anxiety she'd felt upon waking. But where was she? The trees, the buildings, the expanse of green mall ... so familiar, yet ... She looked down at her bare feet on the warm sidewalk. She'd run off without her slippers. "Oh, how silly."

A young woman approached. Mara pulled her robe closer, embarrassed at being seen after the awful thing that had happened to her—and barefooted, too.

"Dear, what are you doing out so early and still in your nightie?"

"I, um … " Mara didn't know how much to tell her. She'd never told anyone about Burian, with his long, smelly old robes and scraggly beard. His messy, thick black hair piled on top of his head and tied in a knot. He was ugly, worse than ugly, a deranged rapist and killer.

The young woman seemed kindly but perhaps she only wanted to snoop. She wore neat clothing, an orange shirt and white shorts, like someone else Mara had seen recently, only she couldn't remember who or where. Should she tell this stranger about the ragged man, what he'd done?

"I think there's a bad person hiding around here," she said. "You must be careful, because you are young and pretty. He's a very bad man."

"I understand, dear." The young woman took Mara's hand. "Let's check your apartment to see if it's safe now."

"What is your name?"

"Diana. I'm one of the night duty supervisors and don't often get out of the office to meet the residents. I'm working a double shift today, so I came out for a break. Thought I'd like to meet some of you folks who live here."

"I don't *live* here," Mara protested. "I was brought here by a terrible, cruel man and then he … and then I saw him choke another man … and then I was afraid he would come to hurt me again. I ran away, and I've been hiding."

"And when did this happen?"

"I don't know. It was dark. I woke up in this strange place."

"I see," Diana nodded. "Well, let's get you a hot shower and some fresh clothing."

Mara wondered why the young woman didn't show alarm by what she had to say. She shrugged. "That would be good, I guess."

Mara followed as Diana led her into a building and onto an elevator. Diana unlocked a door in the hallway and entered first, switching on lamps before checking the living area and bedroom. "All clear. No one here."

"Oh, thank goodness," Mara whispered. She looked around the apartment. "This is a nice little place."

"I'm glad you like it. Make yourself comfortable."

Mara opened a bedroom closet, stunned to see familiar clothing, just her size. "Who on earth lives here?"

"It doesn't matter. She's away right now, but she'll be back and you'll like her. Let's get going with that shower. First, though ..." Diana took a vial of tablets from her pocket and poured a glass of water. "Here's a little pill to make you feel more at ease."

✵ ✵ ✵

Mara awoke rested. The clock showed noon, and she was hungry. She dressed quickly and hurried downstairs. She was surprised to find the nice gentleman she'd visited with—yesterday, was it?—strolling along the mall's sidewalk leading to the dining hall.

He caught up with her and laced his arm through hers. "Did you sleep all right after that ugly experience, Mara?"

She peered at him. *What ugly experience?* She felt foggy from sleeping so late, wished she could remember his name. "I only woke up a little while ago, but I slept very well." She liked the closeness of this man. She felt she could trust him. It was a good feeling to have a man, a nice man, in charge after these years of loneliness following Chet's death. She spotted a name badge he wore on his shirt pocket. Garrick Thomas. *Garrick, yes, that's his name.* She relaxed a little.

"I was surprised to find you gone when I arose early."

Mara choked. Had she spent the night with Garrick? What was going on? She shuddered at the thought that they'd shared what he called an ugly experience. "Oh, my," she sighed. "Maybe we could talk about last night later."

"Very well. I started over to look for you this morning, but a pretty young woman named Diana was leaving your apartment and told me you were napping."

"Diana? I don't know a Diana."

"She said you'd had a bad dream and needed to rest."

"I don't know ... I have such trouble remembering names at times ... Garrick. And not just names."

He laughed. "We all do, my dear. It's why we're here. That's the only thing you *need* to remember."

Mara sighed. "That we can't remember anything?"

"Quite."

They entered the dining room set with colorful linen tablecloths and napkins carrying out the tropical theme. The hostess seated them by a window overlooking the grandeur of the turquoise bay and the dark line of the horizon hinting at exotic seas beyond. Garrick held Mara's chair as she settled into her place.

"How beautiful," Mara said, her eyes feasting on the view. I never tire of looking at the ocean."

Garrick raised a quizzical eyebrow. "Better than Arizona, eh?"

Mara busied herself with the menu. "It's different, that's all." She wondered how he knew about Arizona.

"Different, yes," Garrick muttered. "We could be in padded cells, they tell me." He looked over the sheet of daily specials. "Good! We can have grouper today. My favorite and look here! Lobster bisque."

Mara smiled, also pleased with the offerings. "I'll have the fresh stone crab with drawn butter." She set aside the menu and looked across at Garrick. "You seem like a very good man, and I'll be grateful to have you for a friend."

The waitress approached their table. "Are you ready to order?"

"Indeed, we are," Garrick said and proceeded to order for both.

After the waitress stepped away, the two sat mutely, awaiting the first course. Garrick finally broke the silence. "What type of books did you write, Mara?"

She felt self-conscious about answering this man of obvious intellect. He would think what she had to say was too far beneath his lofty accomplishments. "I began with children's fiction, but on the sly I branched into horror novels."

"Good for you. That's my genre, too, though I think now that I may have over-taxed my brain. Sometimes I have flashbacks, find myself living with the characters as though they were real people. Have you ever done that?"

"I … I'm not sure." Before her loomed the image of the ragged, filthy man, the rapist Burian, the villain of her last novel and the only one she'd set in seventeenth-century Russia. Mara closed her eyes, shook her head to rid herself of the unwanted vision. With a tentative laugh, she said, "Perhaps I should have stuck with children's stories."

"Nonsense. I'd like to read your books. Have you any with you on the island?"

"A few."

"Then perhaps you'll lend me one or two. I'd like for you to read my books as well."

"I'd be pleased to read your books, Garrick."

Their conversation halted again when the bisque arrived, quickly followed by the entrees.

"How is the stone crab?" Garrick asked.

"Delicious." Mara delicately pried the sweet white flesh from the shell with a seafood fork and dipped the morsels in drawn butter. She looked up into Garrick's solemn blue eyes and grinned apologetically. "I know. You're thinking all this butter will make me fat."

"Not what I was thinking at all, dear girl. I was eyeing the tidbit with envy. Besides, you can stand a little rounding out."

Mara looked down, felt her face redden, as she continued to work the meat from the shell.

"Now I've embarrassed you," Garrick apologized. "I should learn tact, but I'm afraid it's too late in life for this old fogey to learn much of anything new. Forgive me, please."

"There is nothing to forgive. You are an honest, forthright man, and I like that."

"Thank you. My grouper is fine, too, as expected. The superb cuisine this 'resort' advertises is not a lie."

That settled, they finished the entrees and ordered dessert.

"Here you go." The waitress set before them generous servings of cream puffs drizzled with chocolate sauce.

Mara looked over at Garrick and giggled. "This will round out both of us."

"No doubt." Garrick hoisted a forkful, which he dispatched with a satisfied smile.

After lunch, as they left the dining room, he suggested a stroll to sit again by the sea as they had done the previous day.

"I would enjoy that, but my daughter will arrive shortly. She'll be worried if she can't find me."

"Come now, we won't be that long or that far off. And what if she doesn't show up?"

"Lauren *will* be here … but all right. I'll go for a little while."

"Good-O. Shall we then?" Garrick once again took her arm.

"I wish I had a bird book and one that identified flowers and trees," Mara said.

"I'm sure the library here has something along those lines. I'll try to find one for next time."

They walked until finally settling on a bench at the edge of the cliff, the bench where they'd first enjoyed one another's company.

"Tell me about your favorite character." Garrick's eyes followed the flight of a seagull as he took Mara's hand in his large, soft paw.

Mara laughed. "I'll tell you mine, if you'll tell me yours."

"I asked first."

"My, don't we sound like a pair of old sillies."

"We *are* old sillies," Garrick assured her, "so let's enjoy the happy state. Now, describe your most memorable character, good or bad."

"Well, he was very bad. Evil. Ugly. Dirty—never took a bath, just rolled around in the dirt like birds do to get rid of their nits."

"My, my. It's hard to believe a lovely little woman like you would dream up such a creature, then have to live with him day and night for months, years even. There is much about you that isn't revealed on the surface. Tell me more."

"Well, I'm pleased to hear I'm not an easy read." She paused to consider how much of her inner feelings she felt ready to divulge to someone she scarcely knew, though he seemed genuinely nice. "I don't know why I became fixated on psychological grotesques, but I find them fascinating. I think I first became interested in such types from reading Robert Browning. I've long admired the intensity, the immediacy of his narrative poetry. He also wrote very dark verse at times, plumbing the madness of men's souls. Women's, too."

"How so? I haven't read Browning since school days. I remember 'The Pied Piper of Hamelin.' Now *that* took a lot of screwball imagination. Very effective, though, as a parable to teach our young the value of paying obligations."

"Have you never read 'Ivàn Ivànovich'? How do you suppose a mother could throw her children from a sleigh, toss them into the snow for ravening wolves to devour so she might reach her husband in another town that night? *He* must have been something! Or 'Porphyria's Lover,' where the lover plots to strangle the young woman who lies beside him, strangle her with her own hair."

Garrick grunted. "I have to admit I'm lacking in my education. Have you known such people in real life?"

"Heavens, no. I wouldn't associate with people like that!"

"Then how do you know they exist?"

"You know as well as I—we can't escape reading real-life horror stories in the newspapers and magazines. I couldn't make up gruesome tales worse than accounts we've read daily for years—and they seem to be getting worse."

"So true," Garrick agreed. "And with a highly developed imagination, it isn't difficult to extrapolate evil into action for your characters."

"I hope it's that. I have such terrible visions at times. I'd hate to think I'm just plain crazy."

"You describe my inner thoughts as well."

Mara pondered his meaning, wondering if Garrick really had flashbacks to his evil characters, or if he was merely jollying her along.

After a long silence, Garrick finally said, "You know, we still have to go to the office to file a formal report about last night's ... event."

"Event? Remind me, please. What exactly happened last night?" She wasn't sure she wanted to know.

"Dear lady, I don't like to remind you of this gruesome thing, but we have to confirm our report about the man we both saw beaten and probably strangled. And that you saw his body removed."

"Strangled." Mara closed her eyes. "Yes, it's coming back to me now. I saw a terrible thing. I wonder who he was."

"And who performed the foul deed. I'm sure we weren't believed by the night manager."

Mara felt the beginnings of a headache and now the rich seafood lay heavy on her stomach. "I don't understand why not. It was dark, but the moon was bright enough to cast shadows."

Garrick stood up and pulled Mara to her feet. "As charming as I find your company, we must get on with this report."

Mara's wisps of memory and the need for the report made her uncomfortable. "I haven't heard you tell about your characters."

"We'll have time for my characters later."

"I hope so."

Garrick led her to the administrative offices, though several times she balked, saying, "I don't want to go over this again. We told them all we know, didn't we? Can't this wait?"

When she stopped again before entering the office, Garrick propelled her by the elbow through the doorway and forward to the front desk.

"I don't know why I need to say more," Mara fussed. "It should be in that young man ... whatsis name's ... report. I don't want to think about this any more."

Garrick told the pretty young desk clerk, Sheila, why they had come and asked to see the manager.

Sheila called on the intercom to announce their arrival to Stan Dickerson, the clinic's administrator. "He said to go right in." She opened the door to usher them through.

Following the handshaking formalities and with everyone seated, Dickerson began, "We have several unusual reports of nighttime activities. I'd like to hear from you both."

Trying to place his accent, Mara thought he was not British, maybe from Boston. She studied the thin-faced, freckled man in his late forties. A man, she thought, trying to look the part of an official, but uncomfortable, like he was wearing someone else's clothing, maybe even dying his slick-backed hair that reddish color. "I haven't met you before, Mr. Dickerson. Are you new here?"

"I beg your pardon, ma'am. I'm Dr. Dickerson, and I enrolled you several months ago."

Mara gasped. "Several months? Where have I been? I-I think I've only been here a few days."

Dickerson gave her a patient smile. "You were ill when you reached us. You've been under heavy medication until now. Don't be concerned. It's something that happens around here."

"Indeed," Garrick growled.

"Now, let's get on with the reports," Dickerson said. "Who wants to go first?"

"I will," Garrick offered. "I saw scuffling on the mall in the middle of the night. When I looked closer, I could see two men in a violent struggle. I shouted at them to stop, but they ignored me."

"You saw them in the dark. The report the night supervisor wrote said the time was around three a.m." Dickerson shuffled papers.

Mara interrupted, remembering now. "The moon was very bright. And there was lamplight along the sidewalk."

"Yes, ma'am." Dickerson turned back to Garrick. "What happened? Did you go out to where the men fought?"

Garrick confessed what he called cowardice in going back to bed, after yelling at the men to stop.

Mara picked up the narration. "I heard this gentleman's shout. I looked out and saw two men fighting. Later, I saw Kyle, that new young attendant, drag the unconscious man away." Annoyed at having to relive this incident to someone who looked skeptical, she shrugged. "I told all this last night."

Dickerson shook his head. "You could see this and identify the attendant in the moonlight?"

"And lamplight! It was bright enough to see shadows." Mara wanted to scream. "Don't you believe me? What's wrong with you people?"

Garrick added, "Who exactly are the crazies here? The lady told you what she saw, and I have confirmed it. Isn't that good enough?"

"Have you interviewed Kyle?" Mara tried to control her rage.

"Of course. I'm sorry to have to put you through this again, ma'am, but we're only doing our jobs here. We have to be fair to our employees when we receive unconfirmed reports."

"How many confirmations do you need?" Garrick asked. "You have two. Have the Cayman authorities been notified?"

"They will be, in time, once we establish the facts. So far, we haven't found the injured man."

"Injured? I'll say." Mara felt at a loss to convince the stubborn official. "I'm sure the poor man was dead."

"But you have no certain knowledge of that, nor do you know whether the men were merely involved in horseplay, do you?" Dickerson asked. "Thus far, we have no evidence of anything whatsoever happening."

"What about the report to that idiot Jerry?" Garrick asked.

"You were both on your evening medications. Right?"

Mara and Garrick exchanged glances and nodded affirmatively.

"Then this action could have resulted from a dream?" Dickerson suggested.

"Both of us? Sharing a dream? Ridiculous." Mara stood up. "I'm through with this *interrogation*."

"Right on, old girl. Let's clear out of here," Garrick rose and leaned on Dickerson's desk. "Let us know when the Cayman investigators arrive. We shall wish to speak with them."

"You may be certain I will do just that." Dickerson snapped his file shut.

As Garrick opened the door to usher Mara from the room, the outer door burst open. Lauren raced to the clerk's desk. "I'm looking for my mother."

Mara gave Garrick a smug little smile. "You see? I told you she'd come. She'll make them believe us."

Chapter

FOUR

LAUREN'S EARLY MORNING FLIGHT from New York to Encantadora Island had taken her from JFK to Miami International. She loved the thrill of flying, of looking down on the busyness of the world she'd left below. She'd leaned her head against the cool plastic wall of the airliner cabin, gazed down at the dark blue water thirty-eight thousand feet below. So serene and restful. She closed her eyes. Escaped.

Minutes later, it seemed—though three hours in reality—she heard, "Fasten your seatbelts. We're beginning our descent." The ocean below had changed to the sparkling aqua hues of the shallow coastline, and she could now see the shore and white buildings of Miami Beach.

She wished she were returning to the Art Deco District of South Beach where she'd vacationed a year ago, feeling so alive amid the bustle then with the reggae music and the pungency of the streets. The rhythms of Calypso always lifted her spirits. She loved the stucco pastels of the buildings with their Twenties and Thirties architecture blending the galleries, cafés and antique stores into their own special ambience.

How carefree and renewed she had felt then after the bitter breakup of her marriage. David had been such a shit. The casual beach life, so remote from Manhattan for that one week, exposed the fallacy that her life must be consumed with the duties and rigid hours of juggling both career and household. Forget sleep. She realized then what a robot she'd become, bending to the demands of her husband and her employment. In the case of David and the divorce, change took care of itself—as long as she didn't let herself fall into one more domineering relationship. She was in no hurry to find another man to complicate her life.

She'd found it less easy to back off from the other responsibilities in her life. Intending to quit her job as senior editor at a small Manhattan publishing house, she planned to use a portion of her divorce settlement for travel, to see parts of the world she knew only from reading. She would maybe do some writing of her own, start with a few travel articles.

But those dreams withered when she arrived home and found two messages on her answering machine. She'd meant to turn it off so no one would expect a return call.

✵ ✵ ✵

At Miami International, Lauren made a smooth change for her seventy-minute flight to Grand Cayman. She would have little time to spare at George Town if she were to catch the early afternoon catamaran transport to Encantadora. With only two schedules a day, if she missed the one-thirty boat, she'd have to wait overnight for the morning shuttle. The clinic's tiny island, too small in area for recognition as belonging to the Cayman Island group, was included under British governance but with limited services.

Pleased at first with the easy transition to the Boeing 737, she began to fret after a delay of twenty minutes past the scheduled departure. What or who were they waiting for? She hoped she wouldn't regret declining her travel agent's suggestion for an advance reservation at a George Town hotel, "Just in case ..." At the time, Lauren was too eager to reach her destination to consider staying overnight in the island capital. A contingency plan would have been wise, however. At least her travel agent had provided a list of acceptable hotels if she missed the connection.

Finally, a well-dressed businessman boarded and the door quickly closed. Lauren thought he must be someone very important to rate such a lengthy wait. He obviously wasn't the president of the United States or the British prime minister, but they were the only two she could think of who rated such a delay. She purchased a tuna salad sandwich but declined the complimentary Tortuga rum punch. She considered the miniature bottles of vodka in her purse that she'd purchased while waiting to board the flight out of New York. No, she would need to keep a clear head.

Lauren looked around at the other passengers. Most sharing economy class with her appeared to be vacationers en route to the scenic islands. A few business travelers were among them, and a couple of well-dressed Black businessmen in the row ahead sat across the aisle from one another talking sales strategy. She looked at the bag of manuscripts under her feet. Feeling a little guilty about the long nap on the Miami flight when she should have been making better use of her time, she dragged out a manuscript and began to read.

Her eyes moved over the words but her mind traveled back to the phone calls awaiting her return from last year's vacation. The calls that changed her life in ways she neither welcomed nor could deny. At least her resolve to travel to exotic locations was being met, if not for the right reasons.

❋ ❋ ❋

The first call had been from her mother, Mara. Widowed these past three years, Mara insisted on living alone in her condo near Tucson. Whenever Lauren protested, begging her to move closer, even to share her apartment now that she, too, was single, Mara found a myriad of reasons why she was safer, healthier and definitely happier living in the desert near her friends. Lauren respected her mother's reasons, though she herself thrived on city life and the more-or-less isolation of apartment dwelling.

Mara sounded frantic. "Lauren, I can't find the airline tickets you sent. We're supposed to be in New York tomorrow, and I've torn the house apart. Please call me right away."

The recorder voice came on, "Friday, nine-oh-seven p.m." The day Lauren had flown to Miami, a week earlier.

Lauren pushed the button to ring her mother's Tucson number. What was Mara talking about? What ticket? *Did she arrive here alone when I was gone? Oh, God, tell me that didn't happen.*

The phone rang and rang with no answer.

She pushed the message button to hear the second caller, doubtless her mother calling back with an explanation.

Wrong.

A pleasant but formal voice said, “Mrs. Hale, please call the administrator of the Desert Lily Care Center as soon as possible.” The call had been recorded six days ago.

Lauren scribbled the information on a notepad and quickly punched the buttons. Her nervous fingers resulted in a wrong number.

“Slow down,” she breathed. “It’s a care center, not a hospital. But what does that mean?” She felt a tension headache building up.

Redialing and finally connecting with the care center’s administrator, a Mrs. Winbourne, Lauren discovered that her fears were well founded.

“A week ago, your mother was picked up at a Seven Eleven in her nightgown, three a.m. She said she was looking for her husband because he had taken off with their tickets to go somewhere. New York, I think. This is second-hand, so I’m not clear on the details.”

“Had she been injured? Was she hospitalized?”

“No, the police took her home and a neighbor volunteered to stay with her through the night. The neighbor knew your mother had been treating herself with cold medication and suspected a reaction. She was sure it would wear off by morning.”

“Then how—”

“When your mother awoke in the morning, she was confused, still hallucinatory. The neighbor, Mrs. Evans—you might want to talk with her—took your mother to a doctor. He put her under professional nursing care, and that’s why she’s here.”

“And she’s been there for nearly a week!”

“Yes, however we’ve stretched our legal authority to the limit. We’ll have to release her tomorrow unless you have your mother’s medical power of attorney and can authorize our facility to care for her. We haven‘t been able to locate any other relatives.”

“No. I’m the only one. I can fax Mother’s MPOA in the morning. And I’ll come as soon as I can make arrangements, but please don‘t let her go home alone.”

“We certainly don’t want to do that. Our only problem is compliance with rigid state laws.”

Lauren gave the woman her office fax number and reassurance that the forms would be sent to her first thing in the morning. "How is she now? Has her memory returned?"

"Not exactly, but she's improving because she's on a powerful drug to calm her anxieties and minimize the hallucinations. She's in a comfortable private room, but repeatedly asks for you—or her mother."

"Her *mother*?"

"You must understand. She's living in the past. Her relationships are confused. At times, she seems frightened of a man named Burian. Is he a relative?"

Lauren groaned. "No, he's a fictional character she created."

"I see. I'll let the nurses know."

"I'm sorry I wasn't aware to call sooner. I've been on vacation but, still, I should have tried to call her during the week."

"You wouldn't have known where to reach her unless someone checked your answering machine."

"I still feel negligent. This came on so fast."

"The onset probably wasn't as fast as you think, if you haven't seen her recently. Three thousand miles away, it's easy for a victim of dementia or Alzheimer's to cover up early stages of the disease, to sound quite normal while talking with members of the family."

"There are no others in our family. We're the only two left. Her letters, so rational ..." Lauren suddenly remembered one she'd received months ago. Mara had written that the cleaning woman had been there all day, and the house was dirtier than when she arrived, with cobwebs everywhere and the woman still sitting on the toilet smoking and reading the paper.

Before Lauren finished reading the disturbing letter, the phone had rung. It was Mara, explaining that she'd been overmedicated for a cold and had apparently had a silly dream, according to the doctor, who took her off all medication. She was just fine now, and Lauren mustn't worry.

She was puzzled at the time but not alarmed, though she had noticed that Mara's memory seemed increasingly unreliable after Lauren's father died. When questioned, Mara made light of it by saying memory lapses were SOP—Standard Operating Procedure—in her world of retirees. Lauren had accepted the explanation and buried her concerns. Her own life was such a mess. It was hard to get involved with someone else's problems, even her mother's. Especially when Mara insisted on living so far away.

Lauren had soon put the episode out of her mind, caught up as she was in her own struggle to leave a husband she knew was cheating on her with a younger woman, her own "best friend." Instead, she'd buried herself in work and became so effective she found that she was not only the senior editor but the *only* editor. She was such a buzz saw, doing everyone's work, that the owner let the other two editors go. Lauren didn't care, because the pressure pushed away time for personal thoughts, from devouring herself with anger and grief. Besides, it resulted in a healthy raise, which she would need once the divorce was final.

✵ ✵ ✵

When Lauren reached the Tucson care center, Mrs. Winbourne walked her to Mara's room, while explaining the terms and benefits of enrollment. She pointed out the areas for residents to congregate while they participated in social hours or attended religious services. The large dining room was pleasantly decorated with floral-patterned ruffles and acres of lace.

Lauren noted that the furnishings appeared comfortable in the sitting areas, even sumptuous compared to nursing home standards she'd observed when she'd last been inside a nursing home as a teen-age Girl Scout. In those days, her troop had visited to entertain the "old folks," who were supposed to appreciate the fresh, bright young faces, but the residents more often looked annoyed and confused by the interruption. Here, the décor created a homey elegance. At five thousand a month, Lauren thought, the place should be homey and elegant.

Mara sat in a recliner by the window in her room, staring at a page in *Good Housekeeping*. When she looked up, her eyes filled with hope. "Lauren, how did you find me?"

Lauren's heart took a turn. Her petite mother looked so youthful and pretty—so vulnerable. "I was out of town, or I would have been here sooner."

Mrs. Winbourne discreetly withdrew, saying, "Stop by the office before you leave, please."

Lauren nodded. She'd looked up her own bank balance online to make sure she had enough cash in her checking account to cover the past week's care and the balance of a month's deposit. She had no idea what state her mother's finances were in as an accounting firm handled them, and she would have no time on this hurried trip to get much of anything straightened out. She would take care of the immediate problems and arrange to come back in a few weeks when she could sort out what her mother would need in the way of future care. How she could use a husband right now to help field these decisions. On the other hand, David would have made them far more complicated than need be, resulting in another ugly feud. He was such a control freak—for others. He was out of control with his own life.

"Are we going home now?" Mara asked, her eyes alight. "I'll need to pack."

"Not yet. The doctor wants you to stay for observation."

A crease formed between Mara's eyebrows. "How long? Why am I here? I don't understand."

"He said a couple of weeks, but he doesn't want you staying alone when you return home."

"No. I want to go home now! I've taken care of myself for years."

Lauren knelt beside her mother and took her hands. "I know. But try to be patient. It will only be for a short while."

"Will you stay here with me?"

Lauren smiled, thinking she couldn't afford it if she wanted to. "I have to go back to work. I'm here to make sure you're in good hands. And you are. You look very healthy. Rested." *Indeed, even quite rational.*

"There's nothing wrong with me. Take me with you. Please."

"Let's make a deal. You stay here for the next few weeks, obeying the doctor's orders, and as soon as I can arrange more time off, I'll come back."

Mara pouted.

"Would you like to have a TV in here?"

"Don't bother. I can find a TV if I want one. They're all over the place." She returned to her magazine, flipping the pages angrily.

Lauren sat on the bed, watching as her mother became absorbed in a page of summer salad recipes.

"I have to go now. I'll bring you more clothes from the house. Is there anything else you need?"

"Nope." Another page flipped.

"I'll see you later."

Flip.

❋ ❋ ❋

Back at Mara's condo overlooking a golf course, the purple mountain range and desert to the south, Lauren picked up a golf trophy her mother had won eight or nine years earlier. How lonely and sad she must have been during these past three years of widowhood, in spite of the lovely surroundings.

Lauren set the trophy back on its shelf and began to go through dresser drawers looking for extra changes of clothing and a few personal items to take to Mara. She thought of when her father, Chet, was alive, how her parents had reveled in their retirement years, playing golf nearly every day and partying at least that often. They'd never been happier. Her father had retired from a major insurance company where he was the executive vice president. A financial planner had assured Chet his income would maintain the couple nicely throughout their lifetimes and undoubtedly leave their only daughter well fixed. Money would never be a problem for any of them.

Mara was a few years younger than Chet and both adapted to his retirement after the initial shock of so much togetherness following lifetimes spent busily running in separate directions and with different interests, except on weekends. Then they would have time for each other. Lauren was always included when she vacationed from her New York publishing house career.

Mara, in her forties, had begun writing children's books to entertain her young daughter, at first. No one could have been more surprised than she when publication came easily and with modest success. After Chet's death, she returned to writing but no longer only children's stories. Instead, she told Lauren over the phone a few weeks after the funeral, she had become absorbed in writing a novel in which she was creating psychologically grotesque characters. She sounded shy about it, almost apologetic.

Lauren wanted to ask why she'd care to write about such types but merely asked, "Wouldn't you be better off getting out more, having lunch at the country club with your friends? In fact, are you even playing golf?"

"On occasion, but I've been busy, honey. Writing is a lot of work."

Lauren laughed, thinking about her own work as an editor. "Reading is worse. Some of the stuff I see is so awful. Can't you write a novel that would at least entertain a poor, overworked editor, give her a laugh rather than chills while she's riding the subway at night?"

"I'm sorry, Lauren. I'm in a grim period, working out my angst, I guess you might call it. Your father didn't know, nor did you, but I began writing these horror stories under an assumed name years ago. He traveled often, and you were in school, so I was alone much of the time. When you two were around, I worked on the children's books, because everyone wanted me to be cheerful, not moody and detached. But I much prefer working on spooky, dark thrillers."

"You kept that from me, too, all these years. Why? I thought you were happy, especially in retirement. What brought this on?"

"I don't know. I guess I thought my daughter, the New York editor, would find herself in an awkward position if she didn't like what I'd written. I can accept rejection from others. It's hard when it comes from your family." The light trill of her laugh seemed intended to conclude what was becoming an awkward subject.

"Did your books sell well? What name did you use?"

"The only books of mine that had terrific sales were the children's books. The name I used for the thrillers was Roberta Browning. Robert Browning would be proud of me, I believe."

"Browning? Where does that come from?" *This is unreal.* She'd never encountered anything written by an author named Roberta Browning and thought maybe that was good. This might all be another tale from her mother's imagination.

"Don't you remember that we're descendants of Robert Browning, the British poet? At least collaterally, if not direct."

"How could I have forgotten something like that?" Lauren shook her head, puzzled. "Have you been writing poetry as well?"

"No, no, only novels. I must have inherited his fascination with character disorders. It informs some of his greatest work, among his early monologues."

"Uh … I'm sure I've never heard that we're related to Robert Browning." Had Mara spent too much time in the summer desert? Too much sun could make a person wacky. Or maybe Chet's death had caused Mara to crack. "I think it's time you came to New York for a visit."

"Way too busy. I'll call you next week." With that, Mara hung up and Lauren let the subject of a visit drop.

* * *

Lauren opened Mara's bathroom cabinet to see what she might have missed while packing clothes and personal items for her mother. A nearly empty prescription bottle of cough reliever with codeine was on the lower shelf. Lauren picked it up. The expiration date was a year ago, but the cap was loose and judging from the sticky spills around the sink, Lauren was sure that her mother had dosed herself recently. Was this the catalyst that had caused Mara to go lose her mind? If so, then the condition could well be temporary. *What a relief.*

On the other hand, with the several serious clues that Mara needed looking after, Lauren told herself she should have insisted then that her mother move to New York where she could keep an eye on her. She wasn't about to give up her job in the hub of the literary world to move to Arizona, but continuing to ignore Mara's need for help was out of the question.

After the visits to the Desert Lily Care Center, Lauren returned to New York determined to begin efforts to have Mara transferred to a private care home close to her apartment. Lauren could then look in on her mother daily, and once she was stable she would move Mara in with her. It wouldn't take much effort to change the den into a bedroom. Lauren wasn't thrilled at the idea of giving up precious space, but she detested the idea of her mother being confined to any form of a nuthouse, no matter how fancy it was.

Lauren's good intentions failed in the long run.

Mara was desperately unhappy in New York even after Lauren moved her to share her own apartment. Mara was lonely and missed her friends. Letters from Arizona only made her realize how far she was from home. After a couple of months, the letters stopped coming, and Lauren thought that was probably okay, because then Mara could concentrate on adapting to her new surroundings. She could try to make friends with people she met at the nearby senior center on the afternoons she played contract bridge.

Lauren's pride in her large, sunny apartment didn't rub off on Mara. She was sure Mara would become as charmed as she with the recently renovated midtown Manhattan condo decorated in soft blush shades and lilac complementing the patterned upholstery pieces. The rooms were comfortable and homey. Instead, Mara sat in her bedroom watching talk shows and soap operas or reading light fiction. Lauren redoubled her efforts to entertain her, inviting her to movies and to exhibits at art galleries on the weekends as she could ill afford to take time away from work most days.

When she remodeled the den into a bedroom, she left the desk in place and set up her mother's computer, hoping to encourage Mara to return to writing, but Mara stubbornly refused, insisting that she lacked inspiration. Lauren was privately grateful that her mother had long eschewed involvement in social networking websites, thinking that heaven only knew what would go into outer space from Mara's computer these days.

Mara's attention often seemed remote, even unresponsive. Lauren, thinking her mother must be losing her hearing, took her to a clinic for testing. The audiologist said Mara had some hearing loss, not unusual for her age, but that her hearing was actually quite good.

Lauren became overly tired between juggling the heavy workload she brought home from the office and extending herself to make a life for Mara. One good thing came of it—Lauren had no time to dwell on the break-up from David.

She paid a widowed neighbor, Rosie McNair, to take Mara to the senior center and to check on her frequently. It gave Lauren a degree of comfort, knowing Mara had someone to visit with so she wouldn't be too lonely. But Mara resisted, claiming she'd begun working on one of her horror novels after Lauren's nagging, though Lauren could find no evidence of it. Mara complained about Rosie, "That nosy woman can't ever seem to stay at home. I'd take her key away if I were you. How do you know she isn't stealing from you? And she plays lousy bridge."

"Mother, it's not like you to be unkind."

"I'm not unkind. I just don't like snoops."

Mara often slept poorly, becoming increasingly restless at night. Sometimes she would carry on both sides of conversations so audibly from her bedroom next to Lauren's that Lauren tried earplugs in order to get a night's sleep.

On one of those nights, disturbed and disoriented, Mara awakened to see the glow from the night light as a fire in the apartment and phoned the fire department from her room. Unaware, Lauren slept soundly until the firemen broke down the hallway door with their axes to rescue the two women.

"Burian has set the house on fire," Mara told the firemen.

After that, Lauren insisted that Mara sleep with her and discontinued using the earplugs.

Even that arrangement soon became impossible with Mara's nighttime chattering in her sleep. Sometimes it was loud and clear. Or she mumbled incoherently but loud enough to keep Lauren awake. Exhausted, Lauren dragged herself back and forth to work. Her productivity fell off, prompting her employer, Harry Givins, to question her satisfaction with the job. Until then, she hadn't divulged her problems at home, though Harry knew about the bitterness of the divorce.

When Lauren developed a deep cough, Mara said, "I wouldn't be surprised if you have TB, bending over those manuscripts all day long and traipsing around in the cold and slush. We should be in Arizona where it's warm and you could be outside in the sunshine. With computers and mail service, why can't you work from there?"

"We are not moving to Arizona, Mother," Lauren said and fell into a new spate of coughing.

"Then see a doctor."

"I will."

The doctor prescribed cough medicine with codeine. Lauren, thinking of Mara's reaction to strong medication, hid the bottle at the back of the cupboard under the kitchen sink. She slept like a baby that night, and when she awoke, the cough was gone—and so was Mara.

At first, Lauren supposed her mother had stepped downstairs for the newspaper. Still in a fog from the effects of the cough syrup, she stumbled around the apartment in her bathrobe, halfway annoyed, thinking that since her mother was up so early she could have at least made coffee.

She reached under the kitchen sink for the cough medicine. It was missing. Lauren panicked. Running to Rosie's McNair's door, Lauren hammered, calling out, "Is Mother with you?"

"I haven't seen her," Rosie said, opening the door. "I've been up since six. I heard your door close awhile ago, but I thought you'd decided to go to work early. I was just about to come over and check on your mom."

Lauren raced downstairs to the street.

No sign of Mara. Forgetting that she still wore her bathrobe and slippers, Lauren rushed to the nearby deli, the coffeehouse, the bookstore—all places Mara would be likely to go. No one had seen her. They all looked at Lauren as if *she* were demented, running around New York streets in her nightclothes in the middle of February.

Retreating to the apartment, chilled and shaking, Lauren called the police to report her mother missing. Then she called the office to say she wouldn't be in.

"Your mother is here waiting for you," Harry Givins said, in an odd tone of voice.

"My God, how did she get there?"

"A cab driver picked her up at a street corner. She gave him your business card, and he brought her here. Then he got worried because she was acting kind of—odd. She told him he could forget about global warming what with the streets of Tucson deep in all this snow and that it was sure to ruin the Fourth of July parade and picnic."

"A cab. Did she have money with her?"

"No. I paid the cabbie. Figured I could put a lien on your salary."

Lauren's eyes strayed to the kitchen counter. The elusive cough medicine bottle sat beside the toaster. It was half empty. She knew she'd only taken a couple of tablespoons from it last night. Mara was on a codeine high.

"Keep her there, Harry. And thanks. I'll be right down."

"It won't be easy. She's pacing around your office like something caged."

Lauren heard a crash from Harry's end of the line.

"Hurry," he said.

* * *

Lauren found Harry picking up manuscripts and sorting through piles of paper to identify which pages belonged where. Mara sat at Lauren's desk with her arms crossed, swinging back and forth in the swivel chair. She looked furious.

"I don't know why you let me write such drivel, Lauren. I've worked and worked all night. Look! You can see for yourself." She waved her hand at a stack of manuscripts. "This is certainly the worst writing I've ever done. I'm ashamed of it and ashamed of you for encouraging me! I've never used such awful language before. You shouldn't have forced me to keep working when you knew I was incapable of turning out respectable material." Her eyes flashed with hostility. "I thought you were my friend, but you're no friend of mine!"

"I'm *not* your friend, I'm your daughter."

"Daughters are supposed to be friends."

"I'm sorry, Harry. I'll straighten this up, but I need to take Mother home first."

"Lauren, it isn't my business, but I think it's a bad idea to take her to your apartment."

"What do you mean?"

He put himself between Mara and Lauren with his back to Mara. "She needs psychiatric help," he whispered.

"Harry, she drank my cough medicine. It had codeine in it. It'll wear off."

Harry looked skeptical. "I hope you're right."

"I'll take a stack of manuscripts home with me and work on them there."

"Forget about that. It'll take all day to sort out this mess. Besides, you have your hands full. Get her help, kid. And yourself. You look awful."

"I'll be all right."

But she wasn't. Two days later, Lauren ended up in the hospital with pneumonia. After calling the fire department a second time, Mara ended up in a room on the floor above Lauren's—in the locked psychiatric ward.

❋ ❋ ❋

Lauren boarded the catamaran shuttle to Encantadora at George Town, grateful for the on-time arrival of the flight. As she stepped onto the deck, her ankle turned and she would have fallen had the passenger following not grabbed her. "Thank you," she gasped, embarrassed by her clumsiness.

"Glad to be of service."

She turned to look up at an athletic-looking young man smiling down at her. "You're going to Encantadora?" She wondered if he had a loved one there also.

"Yes, ma'am. I work there."

Lauren offered her hand to shake his. "Lauren Hale. My mother is … lodged there."

"I see." He took her hand for a hearty shake. "Kyle Vinson."

"Maybe you know her. Mara Edwards."

"I'm new but, yes, I know her. I've only been on the job there for a couple of weeks."

They settled side by side on deck benches.

"Is this your first trip to Encantadora?" Kyle asked.

"No, no. I came here several months ago to check to see if the clinic would be suitable for my mother."

"Apparently, it is."

"Yes. Her doctor made the recommendation. I wouldn't have known about it otherwise."

"The clinic isn't advertised, but it seems to me a well run retreat for folks …"

"Not your everyday 'folks,'" Lauren said. "These people are all writers."

"I was told that putting people with common intellectual interests together could be good therapy."

"Have you found that to be so?"

"I haven't been there long enough, Ms. Hale, to form an opinion."

"Are you a doctor?"

"Far from it. I'm a psych tech. Don't have the degrees to be called a doctor, but I have training and certification for helping people who suffer mental breakdowns."

"Interesting. I hope you can help my mother. She called early before I left this morning to say she'd witnessed a murder during the night, and no one believes her."

Kyle turned away. "I never tire of looking at the scenery in this part of the world."

"I suppose, since you're on the staff, you can't talk about patients."

"True. I'm forbidden to discuss patient problems, even with family members." He gave her a long look. "I'm sure she's wrong."

Chapter FIVE

FOLLOWING LAUREN'S ARRIVAL AT Encantadora Island, her sudden appearance at the clinic's administrative office resulted in an impromptu session with Stan Dickerson. While he graciously invited her into his office to explain "the situation," as he termed it, his voice lacked warmth. Lauren wondered at his reluctance to include Mara and the man her mother introduced as her good friend Garrick. The hostility between the two men became apparent when Garrick insisted that he and Mara be included while the pair tagged quickly behind Dickerson before he could shut the door.

Dickerson gave Lauren a brief rundown of the previous night's alleged sightings. He then dismissed the three from further "interrogation," aiming a wry smile toward Mara. "Your word, as I recall."

As the threesome left the office, Lauren accepted Garrick's invitation to stop by his cottage, along with Mara, for a cup of tea. "We shall set the record straight for you," he said. "That man tries to insulate himself from any hint of unpleasantness."

"I gather you don't like him."

Mara spoke up. "I think he's nice enough, just misguided. He's been kind to me."

As they walked alongside the newly mown mall toward Garrick's cottage, Lauren heard him mumble something about "destroying evidence."

Mara interrupted by telling Garrick how mistaken he'd been to doubt that her daughter would show up. "You didn't believe me, but here she is."

"Mother, don't make so much of it. Why wouldn't anyone visit a parent so far from home, given the opportunity?"

"I can tell you," Garrick said.

"Now, Garrick," Mara said. "You know your son will show up eventually."

"We'll see." They reached Garrick's cottage, where he ushered them into his living room. "Make yourselves comfortable while I prepare tea."

The women settled on the sofa while Garrick, in the tiny kitchenette, poured water into heavy cups that he then placed in the microwave.

"Nothing like the good old teakettle bubbling on the stove, nor have we bone china to sip from," he groused. "No burners for the loonies. They won't let us have anything we might set on fire or blow up." He stopped and grinned, pointing toward the microwave. "Though I imagine we could do some damage with one of these things."

Lauren pretended to ignore him, hopeful that he was merely joking. She glanced around, admiring Garrick's furnishings. "This is very nice, spacious. Mother, perhaps you should have a cottage rather than just a small apartment."

"My quarters are fine, dear. I don't plan to stay long. Aren't you here to take me home?"

Lauren took a deep breath. "We'll see. I haven't spoken with your doctor yet."

"I wish you luck finding him," Garrick said. Vowing that the tea was properly steeped, he removed the teabags and set their cups on the coffee table, along with a plate of English biscuits he'd taken from a tin. "Not like home but it will have to do," he apologized before dropping heavily into a recliner facing the women. He hoisted his cup toward Lauren. "Cheers and welcome. I'd offer you something stronger, but it's a little early.

Lauren started to fish in her purse for her stash of tiny airline liquor bottles, then thought better of it. "Tell me your versions of what this 'mystery' is all about. Maybe I'm guessing, but from studying the looks on your faces while Dr. Dickerson recited from his file I sensed that he sidestepped an issue or two."

Mara and Garrick exploded simultaneously.

"You can't imagine—"

"It was terrible—"

Directing their anger toward Dickerson and the staff in general, the two took turns, falling into a natural rhythm as they told Lauren what they'd witnessed the night before. When they finished, they traded kudos for standing up to Dickerson.

"No clear winners, though," Garrick said. "No one believes us."

"Why is that?" Lauren asked.

Garrick answered, "We're nutcases to begin with, and if we act too rational, they pop another pill into us."

Mara nodded. "I'm afraid so, Lauren." She turned to Garrick. "I wouldn't call us 'nutcases', but we get a lot of pills."

Lauren made a mental note to look into Mara's medications. "I'll only be here a few days, but I'll talk to Dickerson. I want to meet the rest of the staff, too. Maybe you weren't the only witnesses who may have ideas about what's going on. And who and where is the medical doctor in charge? I know Dickinson's doctorate is in psychology."

"The medical doctor practices in George Town," Garrick answered. "On Grand Cayman. I've seen him once a year at best."

"And the nurses? Dickerson assured me the clinic hired registered nurses when I checked out this place before bringing Mother here."

"We have a registered nurse or two at the infirmary," Garrick answered, "and a few nurses aides to run around and dose us. The population isn't large, maybe forty or so inmates—"

"Don't call us that, please," Mara interrupted. "We have freedom to come and go."

"—*residents* then," he continued. "And have you tried to leave? Hah. It's supposedly a haven for retired writers, ones who have, shall we say, emotional defects. There aren't many of us here, because it's damned expensive."

"It surely is," Lauren agreed, thinking of the thousands of dollars flying monthly out of her mother's well-padded bank account. Nevertheless, how better could Mara spend that money than to live in the luxury this island afforded?

"In addition to nurses and aides," Garrick said, "we have therapists, a couple of psych techs to treat our heads and a couple to develop our artistic talents or treat our physical wreckage."

"Do you meet in groups to discuss your interests and needs?" Lauren asked.

"You refer to group therapy?"

"I guess so."

"Yes, we have scheduled meetings twice a week in the mornings, when we're expected to be most lucid."

"Do you find interesting people there? You seem to have similar interests—writers of mysteries and horror stories."

"I avoid the meetings. Those folks are too off-the-wall for me. Your mother is the only one whose companionship I've enjoyed since I arrived here five years ago."

Lauren was stunned. Five years and he hadn't found acceptable companions? Her understanding was that treatment for mental deterioration hinged largely on socialization. "If you don't go to the meetings, how do you know what new people might have arrived, folks with whom you could comfortably share experiences?"

"I see enough of them in the dining room. They tend to avoid me." He gave her a sly look. "I can't understand why, a charming fellow like myself."

"What about Mother?" She turned to Mara. "Do you attend group sessions?"

Mara gave her a blank stare. "I've only been here a few days. If I were going to stay, I'd get to know people. Like this nice man." She reached over and patted Garrick's hand.

Garrick rose from his recliner. "Time for another round of tea."

Mara suddenly stood up and headed to the door.

"Where are you going?" Lauren asked, alarmed by her mother's frantic expression.

"I must go home," Mara said. "There is so much to do before dinner, and Mother will worry if I'm late."

Lauren shot a meaningful look toward Garrick. "The late afternoons become stressful for her."

"Sundowner's," he said, apparently familiar with the afternoon nervousness syndrome, even hallucination, afflicting dementia patients.

"That's what I was told. Come, Mom, I'll see you to your room, then I'd like to poke about the complex for a bit."

"I can show Lauren around the island, if you don't object," Garrick offered.

Mara stared at him, her expression revealing all lack of comprehension.

Lauren accompanied Mara to her apartment and attempted to help her settle down. "You should take a nap before dinner."

"I can't go to sleep. I'm worried about Mother. Where can she be? Is she out looking for me again? She gets angry when I'm late for chores after school."

"She's nearby," Lauren reassured her, wondering if her use of the word "Mother" at Garrick's had triggered this reaction. "And she's not angry, just busy." She wished she had something to give Mara to help her calm down. She knew the medicine cabinet held no pills—and just as well.

Within minutes, Katie, a plump young nursing assistant, whom Lauren had met on her previous trip, appeared at the door. "Knock, knock," Katie called before entering.

"I'm glad to see you again, Katie. Do you have Mother's afternoon pills?"

"I surely do."

"There you are, Mother," Mara exclaimed. "I was worried about where you were."

"I'm right on time, sweetie. Here's a little something to make you happy."

Mara swallowed the pill coated with chocolate and smiled. "Mmm, that was good."

"Yes, and you go lie down like a good girl," Katie said.

Mara obeyed by dropping onto the sofa. She stretched out and quickly fell asleep. Katie gently tucked a blanket around her.

"She'll sleep for an hour or so and then I'll bring a light dinner for her. She'll be okay, if you want to leave for a bit, get some of this wonderful fresh air. We're lucky, it isn't too warm and humid yet, considering it's June and we're heading into hurricane season."

"Thank you, Katie, I will. Fresh air is just what I need."

Much relieved that Mara had settled down so easily, Lauren left to rejoin Garrick. She found him busily brewing up something stronger than tea.

Before the first sip of what Garrick claimed was specially imported Scotch, which Lauren interpreted as bootleg, Kyle Vinson arrived with Garrick's pre-dinner pills.

"Here we go again," Garrick muttered, starting to make introductions. "Kyle here is our resident pill pusher, amongst other things." His dislike of the younger man was obvious in his tone. "You should know—"

Lauren interrupted. "Yes, Kyle and I met on the George Town shuttle earlier today."

Kyle nodded with a smile of acknowledgment.

Garrick looked alarmed. "And Kyle is one of the players in our little drama."

Kyle seemed surprised. "How so?"

Lauren too wondered what Garrick's acerbic remark implied. Then she realized Kyle was the young man Mara insisted had carried the body away.

"He's new here," Garrick continued, "but right into the midst of things. What were you doing on the George Town shuttle, young man?"

"Had an errand for the boss." He continued sorting pills into a paper cup, then handed it to Garrick with a bottle of water.

Lauren liked Kyle's clean-cut look, the spark of humor behind his hazel eyes. He seemed scarcely the villain Mara described. She speculated on Garrick's possible jealousy, the old rooster being nurse-maided by a handsome youngster, though Kyle didn't appear all that young. Maybe thirty, thirty-five. She had to think that both Mara and Garrick were on the island for mental problems, Mara's creeping dementia—and she wasn't sure about Garrick, but he wouldn't be here solely for a vacation. Added to the fact that both had spent many years fantasizing horror stories, Lauren convinced herself that the imaginations of the two were running a little wild.

"That's it for now." Kyle picked up his pill tray. "Nice meeting you again, Miss—I'm sorry, but I don't recall your name."

"Ms.," Lauren corrected him. "Ms. Hale, but please call me Lauren." She no longer wore her wedding ring and refused to allow herself to be called "Mrs." after her recent nasty divorce from David Hale.

Kyle gave her a wink and a grin. "Got it. I hope to see more of you, Lauren."

"I would like that." Here was someone whose brains she could pick, with any luck, to find out what went on off-stage—in Garrick's "little drama."

As Kyle turned to leave, Lauren noted the strong, well-shaped, tanned legs showing below his white shorts.

After Kyle's departure, Garrick threw a fit, slamming his heavy teacup into its saucer. "You must not be alone with that man. He may be a murderer, for all we know. Your mother would be terribly upset. Just don't go near him."

"Calm down, Garrick. Please. He was a little flirtatious, maybe, but not inappropriate. I have a hard time seeing him as a killer."

"You didn't see him last night. Your mother did. No one believes her, but you must listen to her. She's a little, uh, loopy at times; however, I, for one, know she reported exactly what she saw."

"Maybe I'd better go and check on her. See if the medication is doing what is intended. I'll take a rain check on the tour of the island." Lauren headed for the door. "I have been here, you know, before I approved mother's transfer to Encantadora for treatment."

"I didn't know. I only met your mother yesterday."

Lauren swallowed the last of her tea. "Thanks for the tea—and for being my mother's friend."

"My pleasure. But, please, be careful," Garrick called before closing the door.

In Mara's apartment, Kyle was administering more pills. Lauren waited until he was ready to leave and followed him into the hallway, away from Mara's hearing.

"I wonder if I could talk with you when you have time," she began. "I have a few questions about Mother's condition and the treatment being followed." *And your version about what happened last night. How much of what Mara and Garrick saw could have resulted from hallucinations after heavy medications?*

"Sure. I'll be glad to talk with you on any subject, though I suppose you should get the medical information from Dr. Dickerson."

"But he's not a medical doctor."

"True, but he's the main man in charge."

"Is a medical doctor overseeing the treatment here?"

"I understand Dr. Stoneham is officially in charge, though his office is on Grand Cayman. He only comes over once or twice a year unless there's an emergency. At least, that's what I've been told."

Lauren decided she should tell Kyle she didn't much like Dickerson and the officious manner he'd displayed earlier in the afternoon. When she'd checked out the place originally, he was long on courtesy and courtly manners but apparently that was all part of a hard sell. "I'm not comfortable with Dickerson. I find him just short of being rude. I'd like to talk with someone down-to-earth."

Kyle gave her a long look. "I'll be off duty after eight o'clock. Why don't I come by and take you where we can sit alongside the mall and talk, if that isn't too late?"

"Not at all. That will be fine. I'll meet you out in front." Lauren didn't want to start a riot by telling Mara—or especially Garrick—that she was rendezvousing with a possible killer.

"See you at eight then," Kyle acknowledged. "I'm off to finish my rounds."

"Yes, I'll see you later." A date with an alleged killer. It had been a long day, beginning with the flight from New York City, but definitely not dull.

Chapter
SIX

Lauren waited for Kyle while seated at a bench along the mall, mustering what little patience remained after the arduous day. He wasn't late. She was early, but that didn't relieve her growing discomfort over promoting this meeting.

After Garrick's over-the-top wrath aimed at both Kyle and Dickerson—seemingly anyone else connected with Encantadora other than Mara—she told herself she might have exercised a little caution. She could have held off getting chummy with the staff until she'd familiarized herself with the situation. On the other hand, Kyle looked and acted like the All-American Boy grown up, so maybe Garrick was overreacting. She wondered for what clinical reason Garrick had resided on the island for five years. He was cranky, but he seemed rational.

The fluorescent orange glow from the lowering sun lit the greenery of the mall. With the gentle wafting breeze and the busy little birds twittering among the palm trees and lower-growing firs, Lauren's anxiety abated somewhat. How could evil lurk in this Edenic setting? *Well ... that line of reasoning isn't exactly comforting. Two-legged reptiles thrive everywhere.* In full view of

Garrick's cottage, she felt certain he would be watching, so it wasn't as if she were all alone.

A few minutes after eight o'clock, Kyle jogged around the corner of Mara's building. "Hi," he said, a lop-sided grin splitting his face.

"Hi, yourself," Lauren responded. Seeing his boyish good looks once again instilled in her a calming sense of trust. *He's nothing like that sneaking, conniving sonofabitch I divorced. I trusted him once, too, so what do I know about men? Slow down.*

"Been waiting long? I tried to get here on time."

"You're not late," Lauren reassured him. "I'm surprised you were able to get here this soon. Have you had dinner?"

"Two hours ago, right after pill rounds. Want to walk? We have a staff lounge beyond the restaurant. We could get a nightcap and something to eat if you're hungry."

Lauren hesitated. She'd had a sandwich at the restaurant after the nurse provided Mara's evening pills. A nightcap appealed to her, but … "Let's sit awhile on the bench first. I don't want to leave Mother until I'm sure she's sound asleep." *And Garrick, too. He'll have a stroke if he sees me walk off with Kyle.*

"I can assure you, she's sleeping well by now after the heavy dose of sleeping medication she gets by late afternoon."

"Can you tell me why she needs so much medication? She was restless at night when she lived with me for a time in New York. I thought the change of scenery to a peaceful island might stop her anxieties about the perils of city life. In Arizona, her home, the pace was slower and quieter, but she was no longer capable of dealing with everyday responsibilities."

"It's common for dementia patients to be frightened and restless at night. Hallucinations of being moved to different quarters or of being children again living with their parents are not uncommon. By medication-induced deep sleep, the patient awakes rested and more alert in the morning."

"It seems odd, then, that she could tell so clearly what happened here last night—in the middle of the night. And Garrick, wouldn't he have been on heavy medication, too?"

Kyle laughed. "Your mother may well have been acting through a hallucination. No one believes her story. Garrick? I haven't been here long enough to speak accurately about him. I was told to keep an eye on him, however, because he has a bad habit of palming his pills."

Lauren smiled. "That sounds like Garrick. I barely know him, but I can imagine he would be a tough case. Very opinionated, though quite lucid from what I've seen so far."

"That's my take on him, too. As I said, however, I haven't been here long. Haven't read through his file. I just take orders until I've been on the job for ninety days."

"Did you hear from anyone else reporting unusual activity on the mall last night?"

"Depends on what you mean by unusual." Kyle leaned on his knees and stared at the sidewalk. "Unusual things happen all the time around mental patients. The unusual becomes the usual. And these patients, these writers, all have talented, highly creative minds, but damaged in one way or another."

"Damaged?"

"Alcohol abuse, Alzheimer's, accidents with cars or from falls—or even from care givers. Whatever."

"I was told there are only forty patients here. Is that so?"

"Yes. You won't see many as those with more advanced debilitation live in the far building over toward the left of the administration offices. Meals are served in their rooms or in a central dining area, depending on their capacity to get around. Some can be disruptive, disturbing other patients. I won't even go into the eating practices of patients in the more advanced stages."

"How sad. I hope Mother doesn't get that way. I wondered why I hadn't seen many people on the grounds or in the restaurant, other than staff. I haven't even run across anyone living in Mother's building. Is she the only tenant?"

"No, a couple of sisters live in an apartment at the rear of the ground floor. Their meals are catered so they don't have to go outside. They're both quite deaf and fearful of outsiders. Taking pills to them is quite a task."

"My, oh my." *Small wonder then that they didn't hear last night's commotion.* "Forty doesn't seem like many residents to support this place."

"Families or trust funds pay pretty hefty monthly charges, as I'm sure you're aware. The fees are based on a scale commensurate with the level of care."

"Yes." Lauren didn't want to discuss finances with a stranger. She was grateful for the healthy trust fund her father had established for both his wife and his only daughter—and grateful for the royalties that continued from the sale of Mara's books. Her mother could well afford this place for years, if necessary. Not content straying so far from the questions that most concerned her, Lauren asked, "I guess you were in George Town last night, but can you tell me what happened?"

Kyle's eyes held hers as he gave her an apologetic grin. "I wish I could answer you, but I've been warned that I'll lose my job if I discuss the 'occurrence' with anyone, even staff, before the authorities arrive from George Town."

"Why is it taking them so long? It's only a short hop by plane or an hour by boat."

"I wish I knew. Sorry. Ready for that nightcap now?"

Lauren hesitated while she took in the enormous setting sun casting its brilliant colorful rays from beyond the cliffs and over the darkening mall. Annoyed, though not surprised at running into a brick wall with her questioning, her inclination was to call it a night. On the other hand, maybe a drink would loosen Kyle's tongue. It seemed safe enough, though still not yet dark enough to avoid Garrick's prying eyes. Worth a try. "Okay."

Kyle guided her along the sidewalk that circled around behind the restaurant, leading to a one-story, white stucco building with mullioned windows and a mahogany door. The red-tiled roof and brick-colored shutters echoed the general architecture of the entire complex.

"Quite an impressive exterior," Lauren said, somewhat surprised. She'd expected to find the employee lounge little more than a hole-in-the-wall. A room designed to keep workers' eating and drinking habits out of the sight of visitors looking to lodge their loved ones on the island.

"Wait till you see the inside." Kyle unlocked the door with a plastic card then held it open for Lauren to enter.

Pleasant reggae music played softly in the background. Two men were hunched over a chessboard in a corner. Loveseats and club chairs upholstered in floral-patterned corals, aquas and cream-colored sateen were positioned for conversation groups. Plush navy blue carpeting contrasted with white plantation shutters at the windows. Navy silk drapes, tied back and secured with large brass seashells, completed the window decor. Tropical scenes in large watercolor paintings framed in brass adorned the walls and carried out the Caribbean motif. A small, mirrored mahogany bar was centered at the back of the sumptuous room.

"I am impressed," Lauren said. "The staff here has it pretty good."

"It's available for staff, off hours, but it's also for entertaining visitors, families of potential residents and potential donors who help support the Foundation. At least, that's what I'm told. Weren't you entertained here on your first trip?"

"No, I didn't stay long enough to be entertained."

"Would it have made a difference in your decision?"

"Possibly. I might have thought it would impact the cost of living here," she laughed.

"I understand it's supported solely by donors—and strictly off-limits to the residents. What can I fix for you?"

"I suppose a margarita would be too much trouble?"

"Not at all. It's pre-mixed but good, and the limes are in the fridge."

❋ ❋ ❋

By ten o'clock, Lauren sagged. Too much conversation, topped off with a couple of margaritas brought on a yawn.

"I'm boring you," Kyle observed, with a sympathetic smile.

"Not at all. It's just that I started the day early in New York." She stood and offered her hand. "I hope we can do this again while I'm here. I've really enjoyed our visit."

"I have an idea you might like."

"Let's hear it."

"Tomorrow is my day off. Why don't we take a picnic down to the beach in front of an old cavern called The Grotto. We can explore it after we eat lunch. I've heard about The Grotto but not seen it."

"Grotto?" Lauren asked. "That sounds kind of creepy. Like something out of an old horror movie. My imagination is running wild." On the other hand, why wouldn't she feel creeped out? A murder had been committed on the grounds. Or so she'd been told by a couple of the inmates, whose reliability might be questionable.

Kyle laughed. "Only one way to find out. I'll walk you back to your mother's apartment while we discuss the picnic idea."

As they left the lounge, Kyle placed his arm across Lauren's shoulder. It felt right to her but … should she encourage this stranger? Though he was scarcely a stranger after they'd spent the evening together. "Tell me about this cavern," she said when they reached the sidewalk.

"I understand it's at the foot of the cliff over toward the south end of the island—and frequently used by picnickers from here or folks who sail in from other islands."

"Can we invite Mom and Garrick along?"

"Of course, but I'll have to get permission—and we might need to invite another attendant as well. I'll look into it, if you're good to go. I can have a hamper prepared for our lunch. Take lots of sunscreen."

Lauren gave it a long thought, imagining all sorts of scenarios.

"Well?" he asked.

"Okay. Let's do it. And please, ask about taking Mom and Garrick with us."

Kyle grinned. "We'll have fun. There aren't many interesting younger people cooped up here, and you are delightful company."

When they reached Mara's apartment, Kyle gave Lauren's shoulder a friendly squeeze. She quickly stepped back to avoid a kiss, even on the cheek.

"Tomorrow then," she said. "What time?"

"Eleven-thirty suit you?"

"Yes. See you then."

Chapter SEVEN

MARA AWOKE EARLY TO find a woman sleeping on the sofa bed. "Why are you sleeping? You're only here to give me pills." She shook the woman's shoulder.

"What? Is something wrong?" Startled, Lauren sat up and covered her bare shoulders with a sheet.

"Did you bring my pills?"

"No, Mom. It's me, Lauren."

Flustered, Mara peered closely. "Oh, honey. Is it Lauren? When did you get here?"

"Yesterday, don't you … " *No use making her feel bad. Change the subject.* "What time is it?"

Mara pointed to the clock on the wall. Seven-thirty.

Lauren stretched back, laid her head on the pillow. She usually was up well before that hour and on her way to work. *But I'm on vacation.* "Do you always get up this early, Mom?"

"I guess so. Or whenever I feel like it. A young woman comes in with pills and wakes me up, but I haven't seen her today."

Lauren climbed out from under the sheet and wrapped up in a lightweight robe. "Mom, would you like to go on a picnic today?"

"Oh!" Mara's eyes sparkled. "That would be lovely. I haven't been on a picnic for a long time."

"It's not a promise, because we have to get permission from Dr. Dickerson. Kyle and I thought we'd head down to a place on the beach called The Grotto by the locals. That ought to capture your imagination," she laughed. "I wondered if you and Garrick would like to come along."

"Kyle? Who is Kyle? Is he your husband?"

Lauren laughed. "No, no, no. I just disposed of one of those. I'm not looking for another. Freedom is pure gold."

"Yes, freedom. I could use some of that."

Lauren, you idiot. What are you thinking? "Kyle is one of the staffers here. You've met him and he's a very nice man."

"Oh, you must mean Garrick, the man I met on my walk the other day."

"No, Garrick is your friend, a resident here, too. Kyle is a newcomer and isn't well known to you who have lived here awhile."

Mara seemed to puzzle over this information as though bits of images were returning. "Maybe seeing him will refresh my memory."

"No doubt." Lauren paused to wonder whether images from Mara's night of terror would indeed flash back once she saw Kyle again. She wished she had formal training in behavioral psychology. This stage of Mara's deterioration made Lauren feel inadequate to say or do what was right, what was needed.

A knock on the door interrupted their planning. "Time for breakfast" came the call from outside.

"Mercy, that time already. And pills," Mara said in a low voice, "always the pills. Come in." With an aside to Lauren, she whispered, "As if I could keep her out."

Katie, the pleasant, young nursing assistant, entered the apartment.

"Are you new here?" Mara asked. "I don't remember seeing you."

"Six years this week." She glanced knowingly at Lauren. "But we change around frequently. No reason you should remember me. I'm not that tall, good-looking new guy on the staff."

"What's his name? Have I met him?"

"That would be Kyle. And, yes, I understand you have met him."

Lauren intervened. "Do you think Mom can go on a picnic today? Kyle suggested going down to the beach, and I thought it would be nice if Mom and Garrick Thomas could come along."

Katie frowned, "I'm not so sure. Not my decision, of course. You'll have to get Dr. Dickerson's permission for something like that. It's a pretty stiff climb, down and back."

"So you've been there?" Lauren asked.

"Once, and that's enough. Nothing to see but rotting logs and a big, old cave. I like the other end of the island better. It has a gradual slope to get to the beach—and no creepy caves full of bats.

"Oh, my." Lauren hadn't thought of anything like bats, but it stood to reason. "Maybe I should talk to Kyle first."

"That new guy? He's taking you down there?"

"It was his idea"

Katie tidied up her tray of pills. "He seems nice enough. You'll be okay, but wear a hat."

"To keep the bats out of my hair?"

"You got it," Katie laughed.

Lauren watched as Katie took a cup with Mara's pills from her tray, a plastic segmented contraption with snap-on covers, presumably to protect it from rain—and bugs. Mara swallowed her pills without protest.

"You're welcome to join your mum for breakfast at the dining hall," Katie said, preparing to leave.

"Wonderful! I'll get dressed right away. What time does Mother normally have her meals?"

"Eight, twelve, and five is her schedule. It can be changed but has to go through the office. Bye, now."

❋ ❋ ❋

Once seated at a table in the dining room and awaiting their breakfast orders, Lauren looked around for a familiar face. She knew it was unlikely but not impossible that she'd encounter someone she'd met on her first trip here to make arrangements for her mother. She spotted Garrick in a far corner reading a newspaper.

"I'll be back in a minute. I see Garrick and think he might like to join us."

Mara looked around, puzzled. "I don't see him."

"Trust me." Lauren hurried over to Garrick's table. His empty dishes hadn't been cleared away. "Mom and I just arrived and ordered. Would you like to join us?"

Garrick folded his paper and looked across the room at Mara. "I believe I would."

"Do you get regular newspaper delivery here on the island?" Lauren asked.

"Regular, but a day old. We keep up on the news with TV." He stood and followed Lauren to her table, where he placed himself between the two women. "You're both looking very chipper this morning."

Mara hesitated, looked toward Lauren, puzzled.

"You remember Garrick, Mom. The gentleman you met on your walk."

Mara smiled with obvious relief. She tapped her forehead. "My memory is not so good. Forgive me. I remember now. We visited and we spent some time together after that."

"No need to apologize, old girl. We all have our little lapses—or we wouldn't be here."

"Oh? I'm just here to research background for my new novel."

Lauren choked. "I hadn't heard that. Have you made progress?"

"Indeed, I have. I awoke from a dream about Burian a couple of nights ago, and now the whole plot seems very clear."

Garrick looked quizzical. "And would you care to share that plot with us? I promise not to steal it."

Mara smiled shyly. "If you really want to hear it, of course I'd be glad to share. It's—"

"Here you go," the waitress said, placing plates before Mara and Lauren. She looked at Garrick. "More coffee?"

"Of course. Thank you, my dear."

Mara heavily salted and peppered her fried eggs and hash browns.

"Well?" Garrick asked. "You were saying—"

"Don't be impatient. I'll tell you after I finish sampling this wonderful-looking breakfast."

Garrick sipped his coffee while studying Mara from under his bushy eyebrows.

When her plate was empty, Mara pushed it forward. "That was delicious."

"Now, tell us your plot," Lauren said.

"Plot? Did someone mention a plot?" She looked around nervously. "Do we have terrorists on the island?"

Lauren glanced at Garrick.

He nodded. "I guess we waited too long. I'll be moving along then."

"No, wait," Lauren said, placing her hand on his arm. "Would you like to go on a picnic today?"

"Well now, where did you have in mind?"

"Kyle, the new staffer, suggested we climb down to a place called The Grotto and have lunch there."

"Kyle?" Garrick's face reddened. "Dear girl, are you insane?"

"I know you have doubts about him, but we spent the evening together, and I think he's on the up and up."

"You *are* insane. The man is a murderer. Or at best an accomplice to murder."

"You have no such proof. And Kyle wasn't even on the island the night of the … event."

"Please," Mara interjected. "You two are embarrassing me. People are looking."

"Let them look," Garrick said." They should know who they're dealing with, too." He stood up, tossed his napkin on the table and turned to leave.

"Please," Lauren pleaded. "Give Kyle a chance."

"I'm sorry," he called over his shoulder, "but I won't be a party to your demise." He marched off without further explanation.

Lauren looked at her mother, who registered a quizzical expression.

"What made that nice man so upset? You didn't say anything wrong, did you?"

"Well …" Lauren hedged. "I guess I did. I'm sorry. Do you feel the same way about Kyle?"

"Who is this Kyle? You keep mentioning him, but I don't know who he is."

Lauren considered telling Mara that Kyle was the man she'd fingered for a killer then thought better of it. Mara didn't seem tuned in to that situation this morning, so why trouble her?

"Mom, let's see if I can take you on a picnic this afternoon."

"Oh, yes. That would be great fun."

❋ ❋ ❋

After they left the restaurant, Lauren said, "We'll stop by the office to see if Kyle was able to get the permission we need." She hadn't seen him around this morning but she assumed the plan was still on.

"Permission for what?" Mara asked.

"To take you on a picnic."

"That's too much trouble," Mara argued. "Let's just go."

Lauren stopped in front of the office. "We're there now and apparently these folks have rules, so maybe we need to know what we'd be breaking."

She pushed open the door and held it for Mara. Kyle was behind the desk, talking with the clerk, Sheila.

Kyle looked up and smiled. "It's all set. I got permission for both your mother and Garrick to go on our outing."

"I'm sorry for your trouble, Kyle," Lauren apologized, "but Garrick said he chooses not to join us."

"His problem then, we'll go without him. Eleven-thirty and I'll meet you here outside. I'll bring a couple of blankets for us to sit on at the beach. It may get a bit blustery, so wear a light jacket."

Outside the office on the walk back to the apartment, Mara said, "Your friend seems like a nice young man. He looks familiar, but I just can't place him." She laughed. "You know my memory, like a steel sieve."

Chapter EIGHT

As good as his word, Kyle met Lauren and Mara with an armload of blankets while hanging onto a picnic hamper. "I hope you like ham salad sandwiches," he said. "The cook was busy, so I had to make them myself."

"A man of many talents," Lauren said, with a reassuring pat on his shoulder.

"And strong as an ox," he replied, "but you'll need to help with the blankets, and we'll carry the hamper between us. It's heavy." He handed Lauren one blanket and tossed the other over his shoulder.

"My," Mara observed, "those must be big sandwiches."

Kyle and Lauren laughed. "I put in a few sodas, too, and potato salad and chocolate brownies."

"Yummm," Mara said.

❋ ❋ ❋

A wide, rock-strewn path led from the walkway along the cliff to the beach below. With Lauren at Kyle's left side, the blanket draped over her left arm, she helped him carry the picnic basket between them. He held Mara's hand on his right side while she took careful steps. She laughed at herself for acting like an old lady.

"You're not old," Kyle told her. "You're mature."

"I'll say," Mara laughed, "like an old banana, rotting on the inside."

"Mother! Don't think like that. This isn't your everyday hike."

"But worth every ache and pain we'll feel tonight," Mara said. "I will, anyway. I don't know about you young people. What did you say your name is, young man?"

"Kyle. And I'm not so young, but I get enough exercise to make this easy for me."

"I'll be a little stiff tomorrow. I sit too much" Lauren said.

"What type of work do you do?"

"I'm an editor at a publishing house in New York. Long days. Most of my exercise is hanging from a strap on the subway."

"I understand your mother writes books. Do you edit them?"

"Oh, no. She writes murder mysteries with gory scenes and frightful characters. I edit mainstream fiction where the criminals are politicians and businessmen—or women. Though I suppose it's an overstatement to brand them all as criminals. Some turn out to be the good guys. A few are charitable and loving souls who only want to perform worthy deeds in this world. Oops!" Lauren cried. "I stumbled on a damned rock and nearly fell. I wish this path had a handrail."

"That would help, though I think it's mainly used by the younger staff, who no doubt trip lightly up and down without mishap. Besides, you'd need an extra arm to use it."

Lauren laughed. "True. Tell me, what do you know about Garrick? I understand he writes dark thrillers, too."

"I don't know much about him," Kyle responded. Mara had stopped, and Kyle adjusted his grip on her hand. "He seems too uptight for holding a conversation, at least with me."

"Oh, no," Mara interrupted. "He's a very nice man. We had a good visit yesterday … or the day before. Recently."

Lauren was surprised at Mara's sudden recollection after seeming so disconnected to Garrick earlier. "Mom, what did you talk about?"

"I'll tell you later, dear. It's all I can do to concentrate on not slipping."

They continued to struggle downward. The pathway had become even more rugged as they neared the beach. After viewing the openness of the seashore so clearly from above, the thick growth of stubby trees and shrubs seemed to transform their surroundings into the appearance of a small jungle. Thick undergrowth crept over the rocky path, creating a tangle of leaves and vines, making it difficult to keep their footing, especially for Mara.

When the three reached the beach without a serious mishap, Kyle spread the blankets on the sand and set out the containers of food and the sodas. "We'll explore the cave after lunch when you ladies have regained your strength."

"Ooh," Mara said. "A cave. That sounds creepy. Just up my alley. Maybe I can use it in my next book."

"No doubt," Kyle said, with a quizzical look toward Lauren. She merely shook her head.

✵ ✵ ✵

Lunch finished, the threesome headed toward the cavern. Kyle explained to Mara that the islanders knew it as "The Grotto."

"What an ominous name," Mara exclaimed. "Does it have a history? Like treacherous pirates storing their booty here?"

"Beats me," Kyle said. "As I told your daughter, I haven't been down here before today. That's the lore passed around, but it's probably fiction."

Mara ran with the "pirates" idea. "I can see it now. Thieves sneaking in from their boats at night to hide their treasure. I can use that."

"It's been done," Lauren said." Sorry, Mom. You'll have to work out a different plot."

"It would be different the way I'd write it," Mara argued. "Burian would be waiting in the cave."

"Burian?" Kyle asked.

"One of her characters. You don't want to know."

"He's a terrible man," Mara said. "And he turns up everywhere."

"I see," Kyle said. "I'll watch for him and protect you. Both of you."

"Can't ask more than that," Lauren laughed.

They poked over slimy, wet rocks to enter into the blackness of what appeared to be an immense cave. Kyle shined a flashlight over the rocks and along the walls. Lauren held Mara's hand to steady her, while thinking

Mara seemed surprisingly agile, possibly fired up by the excitement of the adventure.

As they moved deeper into the cave, the smell of rotting fish and vegetation discouraged enthusiasm for exploration but curiosity led them on.

After a few minutes, Lauren grew impatient. "I don't know what there is to see in here. Let's go back."

"No, no," Mara protested. "This is perfect for my story. It's kind of smelly but that's all right." She let go of Lauren's hand and moved in front of Kyle so that he had to hold the flashlight above her head to light her path.

"The story again," Lauren sighed. "You'll have to tell us all about it."

"Well, I certainly will. That nice man … Garrick … got me interested in writing again. He said it would be good for my brain."

"That's what they say," Kyle offered. "Keep that ol' brain movin'."

Lauren groaned and said under her breath, "That's why we have so many rejections in my business. All those old people keeping their brains almost moving."

"Cold!" Kyle whispered. "Have you no heart?"

Lauren laughed. "Guess not. And I'm ready to turn around."

Suddenly, Mara shrieked and jumped back, colliding with Kyle before tumbling at his feet.

"What?" he asked.

"There's a body. A dead person!"

Kyle lifted her, helped her stand up while shining the flashlight over the rocks. "I'll be damned. You're right. No wonder it stinks in here." He moved closer to the body, kneeling to investigate.

The man's clothing, what little he wore, was badly ripped and dirty. Sandals dangled at rakish angles from his feet.

"Are you sure he's dead?" Lauren asked.

Kyle hesitated while shining the flashlight over the body. "Yes, with considerable damage. He must have become lost, maybe at night on the beach. Could have fallen on the slippery, sharp rocks and struck his head."

Mara leaned against Lauren, trembling and unsteady on her feet. "Burian has been here. I'm frightened."

Lauren placed her arm around her mother's shoulders and turned her away from the grisly sight. The man laid face up, his eyes wide open and teeth exposed as in a grimace of pain. Flesh appeared to have been ripped from his face and what they could see of his hands. "Has he been here long?"

"I'd say no. Hard to say if there's decomposition with so much torn-up skin."

"We need to go back and call the authorities."

"You're right," Kyle agreed. "Stupidly, I didn't pack my cell phone. Do you have yours?"

"I left mine in the charger."

"Don't touch the body," Kyle ordered, as Mara leaned closer to peer at the man's face.

She jumped back. "I just wanted to see if I know him."

Kyle hugged her. "That's all right, dear. We need to leave."

"I'm surprised the tide hasn't moved him," Lauren said, "if he's been here a few days."

"The tides here seldom rise higher than a foot, and he's too far back into the cave for the tide to have deposited him there. He more likely crawled in here for safety and died from his head injuries."

Lauren took Mara's arm to begin guiding her from the cave, but Mara resisted, staring off into the darkness. Suddenly, her piercing scream echoed through the cave. "Burian's in here! I can see him!" She pointed toward the empty blackness, her body shaking. "There!"

"C'mon. Let's go!" Kyle herded the women from The Grotto and up the side of the cliff.

✵ ✵ ✵

Garrick emerged from his cottage as Lauren and Mara hurried past on the way to Mara's apartment.

"May I inquire as to the cause for such excitement? I noticed men running and heard yelling. Then they rushed over to the cliff pathway. I worried about you, and I'm happy to see that you two are safe."

"We found a dead man in the cave," Mara said, still trembling.

"In the so-called Grotto?" Garrick's eyebrows flew upward, and his blue eyes grew round with excitement. "Do you suppose it's the man we saw that Kyle person beating a couple of nights ago?" He turned to Lauren. "I told you, the man is pure evil. You're lucky to have come back alive."

Lauren checked her temper before speaking. "Kyle was as surprised as we were at discovering the body."

"I'm sure. Your Kyle is no doubt a direct product of the New York stage."

"I can't believe he was acting."

As the three stood talking, men began to emerge from the cliff's path. The last group, headed by Kyle, carried a folded, weighted sail and headed to the office.

"The body, I presume," Garrick said as he started toward the men to satisfy his curiosity. "Come with me, Mara. We can no doubt confirm that this is the man we saw beaten to death. By your buddy," he directed at Lauren.

"I can't. You go," Mara said, her voice quivering as tears spilled down her cheeks. "I-I looked at the man but he was—it was just awful."

"Let's get back to your apartment, Mom. I'll call the nurse for a sedative."

"You'd better get them for both of you," Garrick called over his shoulder as he trudged toward the office for a viewing.

Chapter
NINE

A LONG AFTERNOON AND morning followed for those awaiting the outcome of the investigation into the identity of the dead man and how the poor soul came to be in The Grotto. A tumult of commotion had resulted from arrivals and departures of police and forensic specialists. Late in the afternoon, Kyle brought the news—insofar as it had been determined—and asked that Garrick be present.

"The old fogey will want to know what's going on," Kyle told Lauren.

She smothered a laugh. "He has a few eccentricities, but he's actually quite intelligent. And you're right. He would rather hear it from you than second-hand from us." She phoned Garrick to come to her mother's apartment.

"Is there a formal explanation?" Garrick asked. "Or are we getting the fictional version from the perp, as your American telly likes to term their criminals."

"Please, Garrick, just come over and listen in. We're all curious."

"Very well."

He arrived fifteen minutes later, with a strong hint of whiskey on his breath.

Kyle gazed across the small room, his eyes settling on Lauren with a look that signaled, *trouble ahead.*

Lauren began, "We're all here now—"

Garrick chortled, "In a manner of speaking."

"—so, Kyle, please begin."

"The man has yet to be identified. He carried no personal items, no money. What little clothing he wore gave no clues to the origin. The forensic specialists are attempting to reconstruct his face."

Mara gasped. "You mean—"

"I'm afraid so. His facial bones were badly smashed, and the skin on his hands and face was shredded as though he'd tried to claw through the sand and sharp rocks."

Mara looked down at her hands in her lap and uttered, "That's too ghastly even for my stories."

"But not mine," Garrick announced. "The gorier, the better. Tell us more."

"Oh, Garrick, I don't believe you would create such gruesome horror," Lauren said.

"Bet I would." He looked around as if wondering where he'd placed his drink.

"What's next?" Lauren asked. "Have they interviewed the staff and the patien—, residents to ask if anyone saw something suspicious—or might have an idea who the man is? Is anyone missing from this island?"

"Dear girl," Garrick said, "do you not recall the report your mother and I gave to the administration of this—resort?" He glared toward Kyle, who met his eyes with a patient expression.

Lauren turned to Kyle. "Could that be the body we discovered?"

"It's possible. The administrators claim they have no confirmation that the 'event' these two reported actually took place."

Garrick exploded. "That stuffs it!" He rose from the sofa and lurched toward the door. "Good day, ladies."

After the door slammed, Lauren looked toward her mother, who seemed oblivious to the conversation, lost inward among her own thoughts. Lauren realized the late hour of the afternoon signaled the likelihood that further conversation about the dead body with Mara present would be unwise. For once, she hoped the loss of memory so affecting her mother would serve to erase the stress weighing on her now. "Meet me outside, Kyle?"

"Sure. Good-day, Mrs. Edwards."

Mara seemed not to hear him, merely played with her hands, bending her fingers and inspecting her nails.

Lauren followed him out the door. "Is there more you can tell me? Do they know the cause of death?"

Kyle placed his arm around her shoulders and gave her a reassuring squeeze. "I'm sorry you have to be involved in this ugly business. Bad timing."

"I guess so. I will only be here a few more days, but I want to make sure Mother is safe and well cared for before I leave."

"You needn't be concerned about her care. From what I've been able to see thus far, the patients here are extremely well looked after. There's no certainty that the man was from here. He may have been dumped—or jumped—from a boat."

"From a boat? I suppose that could be possible. What do the experts think caused his death?"

"It's too soon to tell. Battering against the rocks seems obvious but no doubt covers up some of the evidence. The forensic experts will be able to distinguish between cause of death and later injuries, the pre-mortems from the post-mortems."

"They'll be able to tell whether he didn't just fall from a boat, hit his head on a rock, drown and then get dragged into the cave?"

"Yes. I need to be getting back to work, Lauren. Do you want to go for a drink after I'm off duty?"

"I could use one now, so let me think about it. I may just go over to Garrick's and help him finish a few bottles."

Kyle laughed. "I doubt there's much left. He wouldn't be my choice for company in his present frame of mind."

"Good point. But I'd like to talk over a few things with him."

"I'll give you a call later then. See if you've sobered up." He gave her a hug and a quick peck on the cheek before going on his way.

❋ ❋ ❋

Lauren returned to the apartment to check on Mara, concerned that her mother's afternoon restlessness might get out of hand. She could call the nurse for the antipsychotic pill the nurse had been administering, she supposed, though she hated the idea of drugging Mara to keep her calm. On the other hand, how good could this agitated state be for her?

Lauren was sickened by the whole scene on the island, the death of a stranger, her mother's increasing mental deterioration—far worse than when she'd last seen her—and even Garrick's strange fits of anger and moodiness. The only bright spot, so far, was Kyle, and Garrick labeled him a monster. Who could she believe? She began to wonder if she should be the one asking for a pill.

Mara had picked up a placemat she'd begun crocheting, a craft she had long enjoyed for relaxation and one at which she was particularly skilled. Now, she made a few passes with the needle before ripping them out. "I can't remember what I'm supposed to do," she cried.

"Oh, Mother, your work is always lovely. Take a minute and it will come back to you."

"No! I don't have to!" Mara threw the placemat on the floor and walked over to the window to pace back and forth, her arms folded across her chest. "Where are we? When are we leaving? I'm tired of this hotel."

"It isn't a hotel, Mom. It's a lovely resort."

"How do you know? Who are you anyway, the maid? Where's my Chablis? I called for it an hour ago and it still hasn't shown up."

Lauren picked up the phone and rang the nurse's station.

✵ ✵ ✵

After Katie showed up to settle Mara for a nap, Lauren left to go to Garrick's cottage, grateful that it was next to Mara's building, since she was making so many trips back and forth. She found the old man sitting on his patio, drink in hand.

"Mind if I join you?" Lauren asked.

"I'd welcome your companionship—if you haven't brought that criminal with you. Where is your mother?"

"She's resting. She was quite upset by all the—activity."

"Probably the sanest one among us then." Garrick sipped from his tall glass. "May I offer you a Scotch and water or a glass of wine?"

"Thank you, no. I only came for a visit, to ask you more about the night you thought—the night you saw a man killed out on the green."

"So you do believe me. That's comforting."

"I have no reason not to believe you. You and Mother agree that you witnessed the apparent killing, an assault at the very least."

"She did, at even closer range than I. She had better light to see by and seemed quite lucid when we reported the matter to those nitwits who call themselves management."

"I'm glad to hear that. She has moments when she seems quite fuzzy, and in the middle of the night—"

"She had been sleeping and her mind was no doubt clearer than what you've seen later in the day. Anyway, there were two of us who witnessed that man, that Kyle, beating and choking another man. Then he came back and dragged the poor fellow off. Probably dumped him over the side of the cliff. No doubt, the examiners will conclude blunt force trauma." He smiled with satisfaction at his logic.

"Why are you so sure it was Kyle? Could you see that well in the dark?"

"I couldn't but your mother had a good look at his face under the lamplight, and I believe her. She also recognized his 'good legs,' as she described him."

"I see."

"No, dear girl. I don't believe you do. You're smitten with that young fellow."

"I'm not! He has been kind to me and to Mother. I can't believe he's a killer."

"It's probably part of his job description. Off the old useless cattle here and make room for younger while still collecting from the family during the unreported 'absences.' Just bad luck that he turned up, but I suppose it will take awhile to identify the fellow before they can no longer bill the folks at home."

Lauren shook herself at the idea of such brutal conniving but then remembered that Garrick was a horror fiction writer and no doubt a good one. Perhaps this whole scenario was part of his fiction? So where did Mara figure in?

"Tell me why you're here, Garrick. Do you have family?"

Garrick rose to pour himself another drink from his makeshift bar on the patio. "I'd be happy to pour you a toddy."

"No, no. I'm taking it easy today."

Garrick finished pouring his drink and returned to settle back down. He stared off across the green with a wistful look. "I have family, so to speak. A son and a grandson, whom I have never seen though I'm told he looks like me. And apparently another on the way."

"Have they not sent photographs?"

"No. I suppose they prefer that I not become attached to the little bugger."

"Doesn't your son come to visit?"

"Not since he parked me here five years ago," Garrick answered. "He writes that his family at home can't spare him."

"Home is where?"

"Merrie Olde England. You don't think I'm faking this accent, do you?"

Lauren laughed. "I'm surprised you think it's an accent. You might well think I'm the one with the accent."

"I've been through my share of travels abroad in government service when the 'accent' has been pointed out, so I was only making it easy for you. And, yes, you have your own brand of American speech, but it's rather nice."

"So your son doesn't visit."

"His wife, the bitch, feels the need to keep him at home. Contrives illnesses that no medical man has ever been able to identify, to my knowledge."

"But a brief trip now and then—"

"I think my son finds me annoying."

"And why is that?"

"Why do you think? I always, *always* ask him when he's going to get me off this godforsaken island. Maybe now, with this new flap, he'll listen."

"Have you called him?"

"Better than that, I sent him an e-mail."

"You have a computer?" Lauren was astonished that this very senior citizen was computer savvy. His mental state couldn't be too out of whack.

"Yes, and a printer for writing my novels. It keeps me busy and happy." He laughed at the irony of his statement. "When I get around to it."

"Why are you here, Garrick?"

"A mental breakdown, five years ago."

"You must be faking it then. You seem of perfectly sound mind to me." *Nearly, anyway.*

"Ah, but my dear, you are not a psychiatrist."

"Did you do something awful?"

"You might call it that. I burned down my house, accidentally, due to, um, an alcohol-related incident."

"I see. Was anyone injured?"

"No, only my pet cat. She succumbed to smoke inhalation. Anyway, I was sent here to dry out. But the humidity and the—" he nodded at the bottle of Scotch—"abundance of Caribbean resources have kept me fairly well pickled whenever I get too fed up with the place. Like now."

Lauren shook her head. "But you want to leave."

"More some times than others. After the experiences this week, I'm ready to clear out. My son doesn't want me hanging around, however. I'm too old to return to my former employment in the government, nor would I be welcome with this history. I suppose I should be content to stay here and live out my life writing novels using the beastly characters I dream up in the night."

"I think I'll have that drink after all," Lauren said as she stepped to the bar and poured a stiff Scotch on the rocks.

"My only problem with this," Garrick continued, "is that I tend to become overwhelmed with these characters, and they become very real to me in the dark of night."

"Whew," Lauren breathed. "When you were in the government, were you too busy to write the stories before you retired?"

"No, I had begun some years ago. I traveled a great deal and entertained myself dreaming up stories on planes and in hotel rooms. My wife died when I was forty-five." He paused to sip his drink. "I never remarried, so I had much time on my hands."

"Interesting."

"I will admit that alcohol contributed greatly to my imaginings. Sometimes, I couldn't believe what I'd written after I sobered up."

"Did you publish those stories? I don't recall seeing your name in the publishing trade."

"I published under a *nom de plume*."

"Which was?"

"Phelan Powell."

"Aha, I know those novels. I don't edit that genre, horror, but I've read about the books from the British publisher. The stories are written as autobiographies by a monster in a madhouse." She looked at Garrick, wondering who, really, was this man? *He seems so rational, but he is confined to what is essentially an asylum.*

"I'll give you copies, if you wish."

"I would very much like to read your work—and get to know the man behind the work."

Chapter

TEN

JUGGLING A HEAVY STACK of Garrick's novels, Lauren started back to Mara's apartment. Before she'd gone ten steps, she spotted Kyle approaching from the opposite direction, pushing the pill cart as he made his rounds.

"Hey," Kyle called, "wait." He set the cart aside and strode over to face Lauren. "I was looking for you. How about cocktails and dinner tonight? I'll be finished early. You look like you could use help with those books. Research?"

Lauren laughed. "Not exactly. I told Garrick I'd like to read his novels, though I don't know how I'll manage. I brought manuscripts from my office, and I need to get down to work on those."

"Good. That means you'll have to stay longer, maybe a month, to wade through that pile while alternating with your editing work."

"Nah, I'm a fast reader. Remember, I'm an editor. You learn to speed read for survival in that line of work. I'll only be here a few more days but plan to do some fun reading alternated with the serious stuff."

"So, how about later?"

Lauren hesitated, thinking that maybe she'd had enough alcohol for one evening. Still, she welcomed spending more time with this good-looking, companionable guy, especially after their grim picnic. They could probably both use some down time from tending to serious matters. Their previous social hour had helped her relax after the arduous trip. Maybe this evening they could have a quiet time and get to know each other better. Quiet, but not too intimate. She wasn't ready to encourage a serious relationship with anyone, but she could sip a light cocktail—plus dinner didn't signify a commitment. "I'd like that. I'll check on Mother first. Shall I meet you at the bar?"

"I was thinking I could pick up take-out and we could party at my pad."

"Um … okay." She wasn't sure that was a good idea and thought she'd need to revise her thoughts on intimacy if they weren't hanging out in a public place. She knew she was capable of resisting unwelcome moves, however, after taking a few karate lessons upon settling down in New York. She convinced herself she was interested in how the staff lived and, besides, she was pretty much bored to distraction. She had Garrick's books to entertain her, but human contact aced passive spook reading most anytime.

"Don't look so wary," Kyle said, laughing. "I swear I'll be a gentleman and not take advantage of you. Of course, I'll expect you to behave, too, as I'm most susceptible to womanly wiles."

Lauren smiled, relieved. "I'll try to restrain myself."

"See you at six, then." Kyle jotted his cottage number on a slip of paper and handed it to her. "So you don't get lost in this massive compound." He laughed as he returned to the pill cart and pushed off to continue his rounds.

Lauren turned toward Mara's building, aware of a new, light spring to her step, despite the heavy load of books. It couldn't hurt to have a friend here on the island, someone she could reach out to if she needed information on Mara once she returned to New York. Someone she could express her concerns to from a distance. The managerial staff had less than impressed her with the cold attitude they'd shown toward Mara and Garrick. Even if the two were a bit dotty—maybe more than a bit—they deserved respect and understanding rather than a "File closed. Mind your own business" attitude.

Lauren found Mara wide-awake and busy again with her handiwork, a surprise considering the late afternoon hour. The pills must have helped. She'd meant to ask Kyle what to expect from the heavy dosages Mara was given—and whatever long-term side effects might result. Calming Mara's anxieties was one thing, ruining her liver or other organs was another.

"I told Kyle I'd have dinner with him tonight, Mom. I didn't know whether you'd be awake. If you prefer, I'll cancel and we can dine together. We could ask him to join us."

Mara frowned. "That young man? The good-looking one with the nice legs?"

"I guess that would be the one," Lauren laughed. "I hadn't really noticed." *Liar. He's got great legs.*

"Then I don't think that's a good idea. I don't really trust him."

Lauren sighed. "Mom, I believe you saw what you reported, but I think you have the wrong man. Kyle seems up front about everything, not sneaky, the way your man would undoubtedly act."

Mara returned her attention to her work. "Go ahead, then. Eat dinner with him but don't include me. Anyway, I ordered a meal delivered to my room. I'd forgotten you were here."

I guess that puts me in my place. "Okay, Mom. But don't worry about me. I'm a big girl and not absolutely stupid. I've been watching out for myself in the Big Apple for quite a while. If anything seems the least bit out of line, I'll clear out fast."

Mara shrugged without looking up from her work. "Suit yourself."

❋ ❋ ❋

Shortly past six o'clock, Lauren tapped on Kyle's door.

"This is very nice," she told him, looking around as he ushered her through the doorway. "I thought you'd be housed in some kind of dormitory. Do you share it with someone?"

"Nope." Kyle cupped her chin in his hand and gave her a quick peck on the nose. "They treat us creatures like humans."

"I didn't mean ..."

"Go ahead, make yourself at home and look around. Besides this living room, there's a bedroom, kitchen and even a separate guest bathroom."

While Kyle busied himself in the kitchen, Lauren wandered through the rooms, examining the attractive furnishings, similar to the employees' lounge but with floral drapes and soft colors in the carpeting and upholstery. "Your cottage is lovely."

"Have a seat while I pour something refreshing. I've heated up a few snacks. What's your choice of libation, bourbon or gin? That's all I have. I didn't have time to shop."

"There are liquor stores here on the island?" *Why should I be surprised? Garrick has a barrelful of bottles.*

"No, it would mean a trip to George Town, though we can place weekly orders that staff members take turns picking up."

Lauren raised her eyebrows. *So that explains where Garrick's supply comes from. He bribes an employee to shop for him.* "Well, I guess I'll have bourbon, very light. I had a light drink with Garrick earlier."

Kyle frowned. "That old boy shouldn't be drinking. From what I've heard of his hallucinations, alcohol could only make it worse."

"I suppose." Lauren still felt unsure about the extent of hallucinating attributed to Garrick and her mother by the management and staff. "Let's talk about you. How did you come to be here in this out-of-the-way post?"

Kyle handed her a short glass of brownish liquid and ice, which she assumed was bourbon on the rocks. He placed a tray of tiny quiches and a bowl of mixed nuts on the coffee table before settling on the love seat facing her lounge chair. "It's a long, dull story. I'd rather hear about you." He raised his glass. "Cheers. I know why you're here, but what do you do at home—and where is home?"

Lauren helped herself to a plate of snacks and sipped from the glass. Bourbon, all right, and good stuff. She quickly filled him in on her background, more interested in hearing of his past. "That's my story, but I'd like to hear how you landed on this remote bit of land."

"Let me freshen your drink, hon', then I'll confide my speckled if boring beginnings."

Lauren handed him her glass. "I really shouldn't, but ..."

While Kyle poured another round of drinks, Lauren walked around the room to inspect more closely the attractive wall hangings, oil paintings and lithographs of island scenes. Caribbean artifacts graced the bookcase and tables. "Did you bring all this art with you? It's quite amazing."

"No, it was here. From what I've seen, the employees' quarters are all decorated with tasteful, apparently expensive art. Gifts from grateful families of former residents, I'm told—and translate to mean that we lowlies are beneficiaries of chattels no one wanted to bother taking away when their loved ones passed on."

"Couldn't the clinic have gained a lot of cash by auctioning these treasures?"

"Without a doubt, but here we peasants are, surrounded by what Garrick Thomas would surely term modern 'pirate's booty' and, of course, borrowing from your mother's imagined history of this island. In view of Garrick's attitude toward the clinic's management, he would assume thievery, at the very least."

"Lucky you, then," she laughed and they knocked glasses. "What are you having?"

"Gin martini. Want a sip?"

"No, thanks, I'll be on overload with this one." She settled comfortably back into the chair's plush cushion. "So, tell me about your lurid past."

"I was born into this scurvy and disastrous world of ours—"

"Come on," Lauren chided. You stole that from *Tristram Shandy*. I suppose you'll tell me next that you've been riding your 'Hobby-Horse' peaceably and quietly along the king's highway."

"Appropriate, don't you think, since we're in British territory? But I should know better than to try to outsmart a literary person with a line like that."

Lauren was surprised that he used an allusion to Sterne's novel. *He's deeper than he appears if he can spout 18th century literature.* "So, get on with it, say, starting with why you're here and whether you've ever married—or were involved with any other 'special events'."

"Like have I ever been arrested?"

"That's a good start."

"Only once, for smoking dope when I was a teenager, but the record was expunged."

"You aren't a user now, are you?" Lauren sensed again the foreboding that she might be getting in over her head.

"No, gin takes care of my needs."

"I guess that's heavy-duty enough." She was beginning to tire after the lengthy revelatory session with Garrick and now Kyle's story, though interested in hearing him tell of his background.

"I have brothers and sisters in Indiana. Boring background. In the service for two years, Coast Guard as a paramedic. That's where I learned to respect the sea for both its beauty and its treachery."

"I see, so where have you been all these years in-between?"

"Kicking around, mostly coastal cities as a paramedic. I took special courses for certification purposes and am qualified for a much higher-level occupation. But I get bored easily and move on."

"And your love life? I confessed to a failed marriage. What's your story?"

"Well, I'm not gay, if that's what you're wondering. I've had a few flings but none serious for the past dozen years. Almost made it to the altar once, but I escaped at the last minute." He rose to pour another drink. "Ready?"

"Thanks, no. I think I should eat something more substantial." Her head felt swimmy and the thought of another drink was out of the question.

"Fair enough." Kyle left to retrieve a stack of sandwiches from the small kitchen. "I picked up salads, too. I hope you like Caesar dressing." He placed a tray of food on the glass coffee table between them.

"Love it." Lauren reached forward for a sandwich. Suddenly, the room around her swirled in darkness before her head struck the glass of the coffee table.

Chapter

ELEVEN

Lauren awoke slowly. A pervasive queasiness kept her from wanting to move. "Where … where am I?" Everything looked fuzzy. Nothing seemed familiar. She felt her hand lifted, brushed against lips.

"You're in my bed, darlin'. You passed out and I carried you in here."

With vision clearing, memory returned. "Kyle! What happened to me? Was I drunk?"

"If so, you handled it very well, up to a point."

"I had a fair amount to drink but surely not enough to knock me out." A suspicion entered her mind. Could Kyle have doctored her drink? Now, here she was in his bed. She started to rise.

"Wait. I think you should take it easy for a few more minutes. Don't try to move too fast." Kyle pressed her gently back to lie with her head on the pillow. "You've been under a lot of stress."

Lauren resisted. "I want to go." She sat up and looked for her shoes. In spite of the dizziness, she was more frightened of remaining alone with a man she barely knew. She felt no sensation of having been sexually violated, which was a great relief, but what if her mother's and Garrick's suspicions were confirmed? *What have I let myself in for? Maybe I'm the crazy one.*

Kyle sighed. "I won't stop you but, in my expert opinion, you need medical attention and possibly even beyond my limitations."

"You could be right, but I'm sure I'll be okay." She struggled into her shoes and staggered past Kyle to reach the bedroom door. She leaned against the frame to get her bearings. At least, he wasn't attempting to medicate her himself.

"Maybe you should eat something before you leave."

"I'll be okay." She wasn't sure that was truthful, but staying here was out of the question. As she reached the front door, the world closed in again, and she sank to her knees.

"That's it," Kyle commanded. "You're not going anywhere. For God's sake, your mother can't look after you. I can." He helped her to her feet and led her to the sofa, where she fell back onto the cushions gratefully.

Lauren closed her eyes. "What's happening to me?"

"I wish I knew. Are you taking any kind of medication that could cause a reaction to alcohol?"

"Nothing. I don't take anything other than an occasional aspirin, and I haven't taken any today."

"Umm. Maybe it's a flu bug then. Possibly something you picked up on the trip."

"I suppose." *And I hope it's that rather than what I suspect—a doctored drink.* "Just let me rest a little, and I'll be all right. Go ahead and eat. Just not where I can see you. I don't feel so hot."

"Poor baby. You need to go to the infirmary, have some tests taken."

"No! Just let me rest a little. Please."

"You sure you don't want to go back to the bed?"

Lauren opened her eyes and pinned him with what she hoped was a commanding stare to indicate *No Way!*

"Okay. I'll get you a blanket. Can't have you catching cold on a tropical island."

"A blanket would be good. And a pillow."

❋ ❋ ❋

When Lauren next opened her eyes, the darkness revealed only lamplight shining through the windows into a vaguely familiar room. She could make out a loveseat, lounge chair and coffee table. A cotton blanket covered her from shoulders to feet. She suddenly realized that another person sat in the lounge chair beside the sofa where she lay. She shrank back into the cushions. "Who … where …?"

The dark figure rose. "It's all right. You've been sleeping." Kyle switched on a table lamp.

"What time is it?" She'd tried to look at her wristwatch, but her eyes refused to focus on the small numbers.

"Two a.m. and all's swell, just swell. If you weren't so stubborn, you could have my bed."

Lauren thought about making the trip to Mara's apartment in the dark, though Kyle would no doubt accompany her. She didn't feel up to explaining to Mara anything about the evening in the event Mara was awake, which seemed possible considering recent reports. Mara's nighttime trysts with Burian had somewhat been controlled by medication, but now after witnessing an alleged murder Lauren doubted that her mother ever had a full night's sleep. If Mara saw Kyle accompany her to the door in the middle of the night, she'd probably become hysterical.

"Maybe staying is a good idea," she conceded. "Where will you sleep?" Kyle's confused expression told her the answer would be in his bed. "I can sleep here on the sofa. It's served well up to now."

"No, I won't hear of it. Let me help you settle in the bed. I promise to behave. Trust me."

Do I have a choice? As she rose, Kyle put his arms around her and gently guided her to the bedroom. He helped her slip off her outer garments and shoes. She was too exhausted to protest—and he hadn't disrespected her thus far. If she didn't count the possibility that he may have doctored her drink. Too wiped out to care, she snuggled down under the covers.

Kyle turned off the lights and lay down beside her on the bed.

She soon drifted into sound sleep.

✵ ✵ ✵

When Lauren awoke, sunlight poured through the window, but Kyle was missing. She assumed he'd gone off to work. Struggling out of bed, she groped her way to the bathroom where she noticed a new toothbrush laid out on the counter. She smiled to herself. *I guess he's a gentleman after all.*

She dressed slowly, unsteadily. In the kitchen, she found a note beside the toaster:

"I'll check on you after rounds. Hope you're feeling better. K."

Suffering what seemed a massive hangover, Lauren located her purse, checked to make sure she had all her garments intact and took off for Mara's quarters.

Katie, leaving the apartment, beamed a pleasant smile toward Lauren as she approached. "Your mom's pretty chipper this morning, don't you think?"

"Uh," Lauren guessed Katie assumed she'd slept there. The less said, the better. "Seems so."

Mara sat by the window, busily at work on her crocheting. "My, you were up early and even put away your bedding. How was breakfast?"

"Uh, fine. Did you have yours?" Lauren was thankful that Mara didn't realize she'd not returned last evening.

"The maid who just left fixed some toast and coffee for me. She offered to poach eggs in the microwave, but I thought it was close enough to lunch that I'd wait for you to return. Where have you been?"

Lauren puzzled over the fact that this morning her mother at least recognized her, so maybe that was progress of some sort. "I took an early morning walk around the grounds. I have a headache and a queasy stomach so figured fresh air would help."

"Did it?"

"Somewhat. I hope you have Alka-Seltzer."

"Oh, no, they don't allow us to have any form of medicine on our own, even over-the-counter tablets. I guess they don't trust us to keep from over-medicating ourselves. Maybe Garrick has some."

"I'm sure you're right about that. He seems to be supplied with an amazing assortment of substances. I'll go over and beg." Lauren dragged herself off to see Garrick.

When she reached his cottage, he met her at the door. "I can't say you're looking better for the wear, dear girl."

"I had a bad night."

"I'll just bet you did. You can't kid an old kidder. I know you spent the night with that bounder."

"What, how?" Lauren was nearly speechless. However she might protest, she was sure Garrick would misconstrue her explanation.

"I've been watching him, following him to see how far he can damn himself with his actions. I'm disappointed in you, Lauren. I should think you would know better."

"I was ill! Dammit! What business do you have snooping on me or anyone else?"

"Now, now, dear girl. I only have your welfare in mind. I don't want you ending up in The Grotto, like that poor fellow they dragged out of there." He stepped aside and motioned for her to enter.

"I—" She wasn't sure she wanted to continue a conversation with Garrick now. But desperation drove her to ask, "I was hoping you'd have Alka-Seltzer on hand."

"Had a little too much of the toddy last night?" Garrick smirked.

Lauren turned to leave, her anger impossible to disguise.

Garrick placed his hand on her shoulder. "Forgive me. I'm a silly old man. I only want to protect you. And, of course, I have Alka-Seltzer. Sit down, and I'll fetch it."

Lauren reluctantly sat at the dinette table, feeling like a chastened schoolgirl.

Garrick returned with two tablets and a glass of water. "Here. This will fix you right up."

Lauren watched the tablets fizz as they hit the water, then gulped the liquid quickly. "Thank you. I'm sorry I reacted so negatively. I seem to be off on the wrong foot with everyone this morning."

"Most understandable. I was young once and wrong-headed a few times about pretty ladies. I don't suppose your attraction to that Kyle person is any different. Hormones will out. I just caution you to be wary. He's a handsome chap but they can be the worst kind of trouble."

"I'll keep that in mind. You must know, though, he's been helpful and kind. I think I had eaten something that didn't agree with me. Maybe the shellfish at lunch. He didn't lay a hand on me." *Only helped me off with my clothes and slept in the same bed.*

"I'm glad to hear that, but I suppose it really isn't any of my business."

That's a fact! "I appreciate your concern, and I can't thank you enough for your kind attention to my mother."

"She's a dear, lovely lady, and I'm pleased to be at her service. We can all use friends around here. I'm only sorry that you have to leave in a few days. Your mum has seemed more alert with you here. I don't suppose you've had an opportunity to get into my books."

"I'm sorry, I haven't yet but intend to do so today. If I don't finish before I leave, perhaps I can download them on my Kindle to read on the plane and at home."

"Ah, yes. I'd forgotten about the modern technology supposedly available to all of us. I should like to have such a reader."

"Well, that's simple. When I return to New York, I'll send you one."

"You are a sweetheart, but I'll tell Geoff to take care of that for me. Now, I don't want to keep you from your mum any longer, and I have something I need to get at."

Like spying on the staff? "I'm sure you do. And thanks again for your help."

Chapter TWELVE

GARRICK WALKED WITH LAUREN to Mara's apartment, where he bade her "Good-day" before turning toward the office. To continue his snooping, Lauren presumed.

She found Mara asleep, bent over her handiwork and close to slipping from the chair. Lauren grabbed her under the armpits to pull her upright. "Mom, wake up."

"What? Who are you? Why are you bothering me?"

Lauren sighed as she released her. *So sad.* "If you want to nap, fine, but stretch out. You were falling out of your chair."

Mara straightened up. "Oh, thank you, dear. I didn't realize I'd dozed off. How long have you been here? Can you stay awhile? It's been so long since I last saw you."

"I'm here for a few more days, Mom. Right now, I don't feel so good myself. I'll lie down for a quick nap—unless I can get anything for you while I'm up."

"No, no, dear. You rest. The trip must have been tiring."

You have no idea. "Yes."

A loud rap at the door startled both women.

"I thought you'd had your morning meds by now." Lauren started toward the door.

Garrick burst in. "I have just what you need to perk you up, young lady." He handed her a quart of some kind of juice. "Your friend, Bastard Boy, asked me to give you this when I encountered him alongside the mall.

"What is it?"

"Fresh papaya juice. A cure-all, we're told. More important, I have wonderful news."

Lauren and Mara stared, wide-eyed. "You're going home?" Mara asked.

"Not that good, old girl. My son, Geoff, has changed his mind and is coming for a visit. He'll arrive tomorrow."

"That is good news, indeed," Lauren said. "I'll have a chance to meet him." *And compare notes.* She removed the cap from the bottle and poured a small glass of the juice. "I hope you're right about this fixing me up. I can use it." She sipped a small amount and made a face. *It tastes like dish soap.*

"You don't like it?" Garrick asked.

"I don't really care for the flavor, but if it helps me I'll learn to love it."

"Papaya juice has all sorts of nutritional benefits, vitamins galore and is alleged to prevent heart disease, cataracts, you name it."

Lauren laughed. "I'm not surprised that Kyle would know about such attributes. He was thoughtful to send it over, and I'll be sure to share it with Mom."

"No, don't do that. It may interfere with her meds.

Lauren replaced the cap and set the bottle in the refrigerator. "So, tell me about Geoff. Why is he coming now? Did you tell him about the bad stuff that's going on?"

"Certainly not. I wouldn't tell him any of that. He wouldn't believe it, first off. He's likely coming here to go over our financial arrangements."

A wave of nausea washed over Lauren. "I guess I'm still not feeling well. If you don't mind, I think I'll lie down on your bed, Mother, take a little nap."

"Certainly. Make yourself at home." Mara gave her a motherly smile. "After all, my home is your home."

Lauren attempted a weak smile. *I hope that isn't coming true.*

"I'm sorry," Garrick said. "I'll leave. We can talk later."

"No, no. Stay, please. My mother very much enjoys your companionship."

Lauren ducked into the bedroom to avoid further conversation. She pressed a cold washcloth to her face before lying down. The coolness helped, and she quickly fell asleep.

✵ ✵ ✵

When Lauren awoke, she felt worse, decided a flu bug had taken over after all.

Mara slept again in her chair, crochet work dangling to the floor.

Lauren didn't want to disturb her and knew she needed to seek medical help for herself. She slipped out quietly and hurried toward the mall and the office to seek advice.

Kyle, suddenly behind her, placed his hands on her shoulders. "Whoa! Where are you going? You look like hell."

Startled, Lauren turned, shaking off his hands. "I feel like hell. I'm going to ask at the office if I can see a doctor."

"Good luck with that. I think I told you one comes to the island about twice a year."

"Even in emergencies?"

"Depends on the emergency. Otherwise, we techs perform the function, more or less, of doctor, nurse, and druggist."

"I need something for nausea. I took Alka-Seltzer at Garrick's this morning, but that obviously wasn't sufficient."

"Are you vomiting?"

"No, but nauseous, headachy, weak."

"Sounds like classic flu to me."

"Yes, doctor, so what do you prescribe? Are others on this island afflicted or do you suppose I picked it up on the flight?"

"I don't know of other cases, but I'll check. In the meantime, go to my place. Get in bed. Sleep. Keep a bucket nearby. It should soon wear off.

"Drink papaya juice?"

"Couldn't hurt."

"I had a little. Thank you, by the way. It made me bilious, however, so I don't think I'll continue. I was surprised that you'd trust Garrick to bring it to me."

Kyle looked quizzical. "Let's get you taken care of."

"I really should stay with Mom—or try to rent quarters of my own."

"If it is the flu, I've already been exposed."

"Don't you worry that you could pass it on to residents you look after?

"What? Me worry?"

In spite of herself, Lauren laughed. "You don't look much like Alfred E. Neuman."

"That's a relief. I grew up on *Mad* comics and can't always help myself. Sorry. Let's get serious. My pad is free, quiet and clean. What's not to like about going there? Me? I read your expression, but I won't be there. I'll be busy all day."

"Okay, you've convinced me. Give me the key."

"It's never locked. Just go in." Kyle felt her forehead with the back of his hand. "You don't feel feverish, but there's a thermometer in the bathroom cabinet. Take your temp before settling down. Leave a message at the office if you need me paged."

In spite of her queasiness, Lauren suppressed a giggle. *Garrick will go nuts when he observes this. And he will observe it.*

"Atta girl. You look better already."

"I owe you."

"I'll collect, in time." He waved and pushed his pill cart toward an apartment building.

Before settling down in Kyle's cottage, Lauren returned to Mara's apartment to pick up pajamas and a set of fresh clothing. She stuffed them in the carryall bag she'd brought along on the trip, a bag that had been filled with manuscripts to edit. She hesitated, then picked up a manuscript in case she felt better later on. Remote chance, but … She was due to leave by the end of the week, and she'd scarcely looked at the manuscripts since she'd arrived. She added the bottle of papaya juice with the hope that it would truly help, but "Yuck," she said, and dragged herself off to Kyle's quarters. *Let him drink the stuff.*

❋ ❋ ❋

Lauren fumbled with Kyle's door handle, sagged against the door as it opened, then went straight through the cottage to the bedroom. She sat on the edge of the bed, hoping the wave of nausea would subside. It didn't. She raced to the bathroom to disgorge what little food she'd consumed, but mostly papaya juice.

"Oh, I wish I'd die," she moaned, grateful no one was around to hear. On this island, a person talking to herself might end up enrolled in the program—or find her wishes granted. She opened her bag and stowed the juice in the refrigerator, then looked for the thermometer in the bathroom. Temperature normal. "I guess that's good." Talking to herself seemed to make her feel stronger, regardless of its implications. She located a basin under the bathroom sink and placed it alongside the bed.

She didn't feel up to getting undressed, so she slipped off her shoes and climbed under the covers, fearful though that she might be spreading something contagious. "Hardly fair to Kyle," she mumbled before falling asleep.

When she awoke, the room was dark. Only lamplight from outside shone around the edges of the drapes, which had been closed. She sat up and switched on the bedside lamp.

Kyle stood in the doorway, smiling. "She's alive! She's beautiful! She's on her way back to health!"

Lauren shook her head. "Don't count on it. I still feel queasy."

"Maybe you should eat something. Have a slug of juice."

She groaned. "The thought of food—I can't. Especially not the juice." She lay back down.

"Do you want me to turn off the lamp?" Kyle asked.

"No, I think I should try to get up." As she rose to her feet, the blackness returned, and she fell into Kyle's outstretched arms.

"Whoa, are you okay?"

"Yes … no … I don't know. Let me sit back down.

"Now, I am seriously concerned about you," Kyle said. "Passing out more than once is not a good thing."

"I'm okay now. But I think I'll stay in bed. I hope you don't catch this from me."

"Have you had these spells in the past? The reason I ask is that no one else seems to be showing indications of flu. It's certainly not something going around."

"I've never fainted in my life. If it isn't the flu, though, what is it?"

"I have no idea. When are you scheduled to leave?"

"The day after tomorrow."

"I think you'd better postpone traveling for at least a few days."

"I have work to do. I need to get back to New York."

"Can't you work from here? This is the Age of Electronics. Did you bring a laptop?"

"No, and I don't have an iPad or iPhone or any of those i-innovations."

"You can borrow mine then."

"But I need to get the edited manuscripts back to the office, and mail from here is likely to be slow. Also, the chance of losing it would be too great."

"Madam, I assume you've heard of scanners, faxes, internet service?"

"Yes, of course. I'm not completely buried in paper."

"We can make arrangements for you to work from here, if you'll oblige me and try to think of your welfare first."

"I-I don't know. I suppose it might be the wise thing to do."

Kyle's cell phone rang in his pocket.

Lauren watched as he answered. His eyes grew wide and he took a deep breath.

"Has he been identified?" she heard Kyle ask. "I'll be right there." He closed his phone and turned to Lauren. "I have to go."

"Why? I thought you were through for the day."

"Another body has turned up. Hasn't yet been identified."

Lauren sank back on the bed, covered her face with the blankets. "Oh, my God," she breathed. "Yes, go."

❋ ❋ ❋

Lauren slept, but fitfully. When she awoke, well after daybreak and flat on her back, she stared at the white ceiling tiles while attempting to gather strength. She finally threw off the blankets and struggled to her feet. Kyle had hung her clothing in his closet. Nice, she thought, but unnecessary. Her clothing was too rumpled from humidity to benefit from anyone's neat attempts to hang out the wrinkles. She shrugged into Kyle's terrycloth robe that he'd thoughtfully draped across the foot of the bed.

She chided herself for being an ungrateful grouch because after all the sickness she was feeling well enough this morning. In the kitchen, she found a packet of oatmeal, milk and a bowl to stir the mess in before microwaving it. Spotting the papaya juice in the refrigerator, she decided it would probably be a good idea to take a swig of the stuff.

"Yuck, double yuck," she groaned. "I'm a masochist."

She forced down the oatmeal, sat with her head in her hands and wondered if the latest island victim would be on the television news yet. She turned to the local news channel out of George Town and waited, but nothing related to the death—or deaths—was reported. Maybe some kind of political cover-up going on? Possible, she supposed, though without knowledge of island politics on which to base such an assumption. She hadn't thought to turn to the TV or even look for a newspaper after the grim sighting she had experienced two days ago. "What a dunce," she groaned.

"That's not a nice thing to call me," Kyle said.

Lauren glanced up and frowned. "I didn't hear you come in."

"I was trying to be thoughtful and quiet, thinking you were asleep. I didn't want to waken you." He approached and rubbed her shoulders with a deep, therapeutic massage. "Relax, hon' or keep talkin' if it makes you feel better. It's therapeutic to get things out, better still with a listener. Talking to yourself around here can get you in big trouble."

She laughed at his attempt to cheer her. "My thoughts as well." Suddenly, a fresh wave of nausea overwhelmed her. She jumped up and ran for the sink to toss her breakfast.

"Wow," Kyle said. "I've not had that effect on women before."

Lauren wiped her mouth with a paper towel and tossed it in the trash. "Not funny. Did you think I was faking?"

"Not exactly. I only hoped you were so we could get chummier."

"Well, I wasn't and I'm worried." Lauren sat again at the table and buried her face in her hands. "What am I going to do?"

"You'll stay right here until this thing goes away. Whatever this thing is."

"But my mother—"

"She won't miss you. Trust me."

"Garrick? He'll be suspicious as hell. And his son is arriving today. I really want to meet and talk with him."

"Not in your present state. Go back to bed and rest. And let me take care of what you eat. Got it?"

"I'll stay for now. But no food, please."

"Maybe you'll feel better by the end of the day."

"I need to notify my office that I'll have to delay returning home—and change the airline ticket. I can't travel like this."

"I'll call your boss and take care of your ticket arrangements. Are the ticket and itinerary in your purse?"

"Yes. But be careful not to frighten Harry. I'd prefer not to lose my job."

"I understand. I'll tell him you have a bout of something going around and should be back by the end of next week."

"That long? Oh … just tell him I'll call when I feel better but not to expect me there on Monday morning." She found her purse and dug out the address book she always carried. "Here. His name is Harry Givins. And here's the ticket with the information you'll need."

"I'll get right on it. Go." He gently pushed her toward the bedroom.

Lauren groaned and trudged off to bed. She could hear Kyle tidying the kitchen and loading the dishwasher. "Right on it, yeah." She pulled the sheet up to her chin and closed her eyes. *I forgot to ask him about the new victim.*

❋ ❋ ❋

Loud pounding on the front door startled Lauren from her sleep. She sat up, tried to orient herself to the surroundings. She heard the door crash open and Garrick's angry voice.

"Where are you?" he called.

Lauren crawled out of bed and again struggled into Kyle's robe. She staggered into the living room to face Garrick's wild eyes and florid face.

"What are you doing here?" he asked.

"I might ask you the same question." She stepped close and raised her face to his. "Do I look healthy to you?"

"You look a little piquey—and tousled. What has that man done to you?"

Lauren expelled a sigh of annoyance. "He has done nothing but help me. I'm ill. Can't you see that?"

Garrick plunged heavily into a lounge chair. "Most suspicious. Dead bodies turning up all over the place, and then you getting sick. Better watch it, girl. Hanging around with a man your mother and I assure you is a murderer isn't healthy, in my book."

"You have no actual proof that he is a murderer, Garrick." She sat on the sofa, faced him and wrapped the robe tighter. "It was the middle of the night, dark—"

"With sufficient lighting to recognize someone we see every day."

"You were at some distance, so in spite of the lighting, isn't it possible you were mistaken?" She didn't want to add the obvious reasons for doubting their observations.

"Your mother is more certain than I, but she convinced me with the description she gave."

Lauren snickered. "Yeah. 'Nice legs'."

"She recognized more than that."

"Garrick, you know she's not mentally stable at the best of times, and in the middle of the night I doubt that she could clearly identify him."

"Why are you defending him?" Garrick asked. "Has he won you over with sweet talk and wine?"

"Please. I can hardly hold my head up, and you're badgering me." Actually, she was feeling better after the nap.

"I'm sorry, dear girl. I just want to protect you. And I want you to meet my son."

"Is he here already?" She didn't want to miss Geoff, and his visit was bound to be short.

"Not yet. He'll arrive this evening and only stay for a day."

Lauren felt at a loss for how to handle the situation. "I don't want to infect either of you if I have a bug that's catching. That's why I'm avoiding Mother at the moment. And, so far, I haven't been able to keep anything down. But I do very much want to get to know your son."

"And I want him to know you, Lauren. I'm sure you two will get on well together."

"You sound like a matchmaker," she teased, "but you've told me he's taken."

"So he is, and so encumbered with offspring that he finds little enough time for his old man." Garrick sounded bitter.

"Give me a few hours. With luck, it's a twenty-four hour flu or maybe something I ate. I hope to be in good health by tomorrow. Please, Garrick, go now, so I can lie back down and rest. Before I upchuck again."

"Very well, but against my better judgment. Promise me that if you feel worse this evening, you'll ring me. Between Geoff and me, we can take on your captor and rescue you."

"Oh, now, how melodramatic. I suppose you'll swim the moat and scale the wall. Go, Sir Garrick of Balderdash, and lay your fears to rest."

After Garrick left, Lauren lay down on the sofa and snuggled into the large, soft robe. Her stomach rumbled and she felt a slight twinge of pain between her eyebrows. "Oh, rats," she cried before falling asleep again.

Chapter

THIRTEEN

GARRICK STOOD AT THE window overlooking the mall while he awaited the call from the front office, the call telling him that Geoff had arrived. After his son's only previous trip to Encantadora, Garrick knew he would probably need to fetch him. If he was hungry, they could stop at the dining room. Garrick had brought home leftovers from his large lunch, but that wouldn't be enough for the two of them. He supposed he could go ahead and snack on those now, then sit by and watch Geoff wolf down a decent meal. Geoff had always been a slender man, muscular but not fat. Garrick wondered if the boy had developed a middle-age paunch by now. He'd know soon enough.

Bored, Garrick paced, then sat in the lounger with his feet up. Snores soon ripped through the otherwise silent room.

❋ ❋ ❋

The ringing phone awoke Garrick with a start. He fumbled to get his feet on the ground and into the loafers he'd kicked off. By the time he reached the phone, the line was dead. Still groggy from the nap, he fussed around in the kitchen to make a cup of tea. As he returned to the living room, a knock startled him.

Garrick opened the door and, astonished, staggered backward, nearly falling. "Phelan! Why are you here? Where did you come from?"

Geoff chuckled. "It's me, Dad. Not your old friend. Or should I say nemesis?"

Garrick shook his head. "Right you are," he apologized. "I'd been asleep and guess I hadn't gathered all my senses."

The two big men hugged and Geoff pounded his father affectionately on the back. "I thought you'd disposed of that filthy bugger by now. You haven't mentioned him in some time."

Garrick harrumphed, thinking it best to keep the subject of their communication—or lack thereof—on hold. He pointed to the sofa.

Geoff set his valise on the floor and slipped out of his lightweight jacket before sitting. "So, what have you been up to? Are you still writing? Is that where Phelan is coming from?"

"I wish I could say I were, but I've been preoccupied of late. Phelan only comes to me in dreams. Have you eaten?"

"Yes, the flight was delayed at takeoff, so I had a decent meal while I waited. What about you? I hope you didn't wait."

"It makes no difference. I have food here and will eat more later if I feel like it."

"So," Geoff grinned, "any more bodies turn up? You said they found a croaker when we last talked."

"As a matter of fact, yes."

"You're joshing me. Is this Phelan still running around in your head, or is it a fact?"

"Phelan? No, not at all. We've had three dead bodies this week. God only knows how many more have been floating around, if you will, before Miss Marple and I reported the first atrocity."

Geoff laughed. "Miss Marple—you mean Agatha Christie is here, too? You *are* in good company."

"No, no," Garrick laughed. "That dear lady is long gone—around the time you landed on this blighted planet. I refer to a fine little lady I've been consorting with, another inmate, who also writes mysteries and horror stories and who also witnessed the killing on the mall a few nights ago. Middle of the night, actually."

"Good grief. Are you sure you both didn't imagine it?"

"Certainly not. We viewed the—event—from different aspects. No one believes us crazies, of course."

Geoff shook his head, thinking the authorities might have reasonable doubts. "Well … "

"See? You, too. You're all quick to assign hallucinations to us just because we are certified loonies."

"I didn't mean—"

"And that's not all. A body turned up at the bottom of the cliff in a dubious picnic area, a cave called The Grotto the day my friend—"

"Miss Marple?"

"Mara is her name. She and her daughter were accompanied by the murderer."

"You're kidding. Picnics in a cave? With a murderer? Who's in charge here? Maybe I should talk with the director. I gather that you didn't accompany them."

"No, I chose not to join that little party, though I was invited."

"Wise choice, I'd say."

"You haven't heard it all. Another body was found yesterday. Not one has been identified so far as I know. Apparently the poor soul we witnessed being done in is neither of the latter two."

Geoff ran his hand over his forehead and smoothed back his thick blond hair. "That stuffs it, Dad. We need to think about getting you out of here."

Garrick brightened at the prospect. "Well, now, there's a preggers thought. Something good might come out of this after all, if you don't become too sympathetic for the poor croakers. Chances are they were drug dealers or runners anyway."

"I'll talk to the director tomorrow. I suppose it's too late tonight. It's nine o'clock."

"Yes, and doubtless we'll have a fourth body by then. I think I'll have that snack now."

✵ ✵ ✵

In the morning, Garrick rousted Geoff from sound sleep where he lay stretched, fully clothed, on the sofa. "We must get to breakfast before all the good pastries disappear. You've slept the clock 'round, dear boy."

"I'm surprised people are up and about so early on a tropical island," Geoff groused. "Don't they know they're retired?"

"The staff shares breakfasts with us, and they hit the good stuff early. Sometimes, there's barely enough for us poor victims, merely crumbs of toast and gruel."

"Victims, gruel. Hah! I see your imagination is alive and well. You've actually got a pretty good place to live, it appears to me."

"If you don't consider the recently dead. Of course, depending on who they were that may mean more food for the rest of us."

Geoff affected a high manner, twirling his hand in the air. "Pater, dear old boy, has anyone ever mentioned that you can be gross?"

"Frequently, in my past life. I choose not to communicate with many here—or many who could give a rat's ass."

Geoff changed into fresh clothing as they talked. "It's a relief not to have to wear a tie. I could get used to this style of living."

"You're welcome to my place. You might find it most comfortable away from a world filled with squalling infants and a nagging wife."

Geoff groaned. "It's not like that. You never did like Penelope, admit it."

"Well … let's leave it that we have issues with compatibility. Maybe when I return to England she'll have a change of heart."

"Umm, we'll see. Shall we breakfast then before tackling the director?"

"Certainly. We need time to plan our attack. The management here, as with most organizations, I have found, reacts poorly to criticism, so we must work on our subtle approach."

Geoff laughed heartily. "I doubt that there will be enough time in the millennium to expect subtlety in your approach. I, for one, don't plan to criticize, just inquire."

"But, you see, I've already laid a grid of hostility after the disbelieving sonofabitch in essence deemed Mara and me liars."

Geoff frowned. "I should say that was uncalled for on his part."

"Indeed. Shall we invite her and her daughter who is also visiting to join us?

"If you think it's a good idea."

"Mara should be running on all cylinders this early in the day, so let's have at it."

While they walked briskly to Mara's apartment in the fresh morning breeze, Garrick told Geoff about Lauren and her illness.

"Maybe the humid climate doesn't agree with her," Geoff suggested.

"Possibly, though I haven't noticed it in her mother, who was transplanted from the arid climate of Arizona. Of course, that state has its summer monsoons. New York has its share of summer humidity too. No, I don't think it's the climate affecting her. And it isn't ungodly hot and humid yet. We're having fairly moderate temperatures for early June."

"Maybe so, but I noticed that it had cranked up fairly well by the end of the day."

"Not as stifling as it will be by the end of the month, dear boy. You've never visited here in the summer months, during hurricane season. It was winter when you planted me here."

At Mara's door, Garrick raised his hand to rap but found the door ajar. "Knock, knock," he called. "If you're decent in there, we've come to invite you to breakfast."

The door opened wide, and Lauren stood before them. "Good morning." She looked at Geoff and smiled. "I presume you are Garrick's son? You look a great deal like him."

Geoff offered a mock scowl. "That's what I'm told—that I look like him. There is other evidence that I'm his son as well."

"Do come in. Mom is still getting dressed, but she'll be out in a minute."

Garrick spoke up. "We're rather in a hurry before all the decent breakfast servings disappear. You look much improved today, my dear. How did you escape that beast?"

"You surely have a dim view of the man, Garrick. He's been nothing but good to me. And he sent me on my way when I could hold my head up this morning. I seem to be over whatever it was, but I'll wait a couple of extra days before returning home."

"Very good. You are wise to do so."

Mara entered the room with a cheerful trill in her voice. "Garrick, I'm so pleased to see you. And this must be your son. You look so much alike."

"Yes, so we've heard," Garrick said. "I wish to treat you all to breakfast, so hurry now, and then we'll, as a unified force, tackle the director in his office.

Chapter FOURTEEN

LAUREN STUDIED GEOFF STUDYING Mara over breakfast, reading his curiosity about how such a delicate little woman could be the creator of horror stories that had been best sellers. He had apologized for being unfamiliar with Mara's work, saying the mystery genre, and fiction in general, wasn't high on his reading list, while conceding that his father excelled in writing horror tales and was highly regarded by the critics. Surely Geoff must read his father's novels. She was fairly certain she knew what was passing through his brain: their elders were bonkers, living out their fictions, so who would believe them about the alleged killing?

She was grateful that the conversation stayed generally on lighter subjects, apparently in deference to the process of becoming acquainted. When it eventually came around to their real life horror, the dead bodies that had been discovered, Lauren wished she could escape. She didn't feel ill this morning but still fairly light-headed. She wondered how she could participate in taking on the front office but knew it had to be done.

At length, Garrick stood and proclaimed, "The time has come to go into battle."

Geoff looked searchingly at Lauren, his thoughts perfectly clear. They were in harmony. She gave a slight nod and shrug of her shoulders, placed her napkin on the table and turned to assist Mara to her feet.

"No, no, dear," Mara protested. "I may be old, but I'm not feeble."

"I know, Mom. But we've been sitting here for an hour and a half, and I thought you might welcome a little support."

Mara smiled and tweaked Lauren's cheek. "You always were a thoughtful child."

Lauren groaned inwardly though felt relief that Mara seemed to have her head on straight this morning. Mara's unpredictable morning lucidity would be essential now, if the group were to appear credible to the director.

Garrick led the way while Geoff trailed after holding the door for the women to exit. Arriving at the office, Garrick marched to the desk, confronted Sheila and demanded an interview with Dickerson.

"We have visiting family members who are entitled to know what is going on and what to expect about the future welfare of all the inmate—residents of this … island."

Sheila looked up from the computer. She glanced at the assemblage, then lowered her head as though consulting a schedule. Lauren could see she was grinding her teeth, probably trying to control an outburst that might be deemed inappropriate by the management. Or maybe not, in this case. Management hadn't been too cooperative up to this point and would probably reward the clerk with a bonus were she to put the fussbudgets in their places.

"Dr. Dickerson is in a meeting, sir."

"Balls. Tell him right now that if we don't see him immediately two of his chief witnesses to the atrocities being perpetrated here will leave—permanently. I'm sure the prospect of revenue loss will mobilize him, especially with the current attrition rate amongst the head count."

Lauren stifled a smile as she watched the clerk leave the desk to step into Dickerson's office.

Stan Dickerson himself appeared seconds later to usher the group into his office.

Garrick took over. "My son Geoffrey is here from London, and you know Mrs. Edwards's daughter Lauren. We are expecting explanations and are therefore here for a sit-down while you tell us—and our family members—who died, how and whether the murderer has been arrested."

"Yes, I understand. Please be seated." Dickerson pointed toward a small conference table at the side of his large office. A frown creased his forehead, making the thin smile on his narrow face appear to Lauren not just insincere but almost ghoulish.

Mara gazed toward the floor-to-ceiling windows overlooking the turquoise sea beyond, openly admiring the grounds decorated with palm trees and the proliferation of red bougainvillea. "You are a lucky man to have such a beautiful view," she said. "You should commission someone to paint this lovely scene in oils."

Lauren nodded in agreement. "I envy you this view. It's a far cry from mine in Manhattan." Maybe a little pleasantry would go further with the man than Garrick's gruff pronouncements.

Dickerson made no comment but after each was seated took his place at the head of the table.

Before the man could speak, Garrick burst forth. "We are more than merely curious to know what has been happening here and what you have found. Needless to say, we do not feel safe and believe you have a responsibility to assure us that measures have been taken to protect us."

"You are in no danger," Dickerson said. He looked around at the faces. "Other than the report that you made, what have you heard?"

"That several bodies have been found," Geoff offered. "We have been told nothing, however, about who died or the causes."

"That is a fact," proclaimed Garrick, the women murmuring their agreement.

"First off," Dickerson said, "I can't divulge information about matters under investigation."

"Jesus H. Christ, man!" Garrick shouted, pounding both fists on the table. "Are you planning to stonewall us when we've been smack in the center of murders taking place all over this benighted island?"

Dickerson ran his hand across his brow. "First of all, Mr. Thomas, we have not confirmed that the deaths are the result of murders."

"But deaths, you say," Geoff interrupted. "Exactly how many deaths are you talking about? And where were they found? Surely not in their beds. Have there been autopsies?"

Dickerson hesitated. "Three deceased. Or four." He turned his attention to Lauren and Geoff. "The incident on the mall reported by your father and

Mrs. Edwards has never been proven, though we are still investigating. One unfortunate soul was found in The Grotto by one of our staff. You were present, I understand, Ms. Hale, as was your mother."

"Yes, they were," Garrick interrupted. "So it's hard to hide that one."

Dickerson continued. "We believe the man came ashore from a ship, which departed without him aboard. Another was an apparent suicide who leaped off a cliff two nights ago, and the latest was found early this morning hanging inside the laundry facilities."

"Oh, no," Mara cried. "The poor soul. Who are these people? Do I know them?"

Dickerson studied the ballpoint pen he swiveled in his hands. "I wish I could tell you."

"All of these were men?" Lauren asked.

"The latest was a woman, one of our residents, as was the gentleman who committed suicide."

"Have you had a rash of such incidents in the past?" Geoff asked.

"On occasion, we've had two deaths in a day, but they were from natural causes. Most of our residents are senior citizens, so it is not unexpected, nor is suicide, despite our protective measures."

Garrick muttered something unintelligible to Geoff, who merely nodded.

"Who is investigating?" Lauren asked. "The George Town authorities?"

"Yes. This is their jurisdiction, and I believe them to be thorough and competent.

"But the woman who was hanging," Lauren asked, "could she have hung herself?"

Dickerson looked uncomfortable. "That has yet to be determined. I'm sorry, but that's all I can say at this point. We are doing everything possible to protect our residents."

Lauren thought the man seemed sincere, but still … How safe was it here for Mara? She glanced over at her mother, who seemed detached and had been silent after hearing of the deaths. "I hope I won't have to remove Mother to a safer environment. I can't feel right about leaving her where she might be in danger.

"Furthermore, I've been quite ill the past couple of days and wonder if there is a virus going around. Have you heard of anyone ill with flu-like symptoms?" Nausea was beginning to return but surely from the stress of the meeting this time, she told herself and fairly certain she could keep it under control.

Dickerson shook his head. "No, though to be quite frank, I've been preoccupied with the investigations."

"What are you doing to ensure our safety?" Garrick asked.

"We have added two guards to the night staff. They will patrol the housing area. You should be quite safe."

"The hawks guarding the hen house," Garrick muttered under his breath.

"I will only be here for another day," Geoff said. "I would like more assurance than you've offered that my father is safe—and Mrs. Edwards as well."

"We could move them to the dormitories until the investigation is over, if that would suit you."

"Gawd, no," Garrick interjected. "I prefer to take my chances."

"Mom, what about you?" Lauren asked. "Would you feel safer in the dormitory where you'd be surrounded by other residents?"

"What?" Mara asked. "I just want to go home. I need a nap. All this talk is wearing me out."

"We'll think about it," Lauren said. "I'll be here for a few more days until I feel well enough to travel. I hope that will give us enough time to sort out our plans." Which reminded her that she needed to call Harry Givins to let him know what was going on and that while she's recovering she would make time during these next few days to work over the manuscripts she'd brought along. Harry was a reasonably patient man, and she wanted to reassure him that he wasn't being taken advantage of. Though Kyle had spoken with Harry, he must be wondering how sick she was that she hadn't called him by now.

"I guess we're done here," Garrick said, "but I shall not be satisfied until you tell me exactly what happened and to whom. And, mind you, we expect you to find the body of the poor soul we reported."

"I understand, Mr. Thomas, and you have my assurances that this matter has highest level priority."

The group left dissatisfied but not surprised over the results of the meeting. Other than Mara, possibly, who seemed not in the least concerned.

Chapter

FIFTEEN

Kyle hailed Lauren as the dejected foursome trudged along the mall toward their living quarters.

"You left your papaya juice at my cottage," Kyle called, waving the bottle of pinkish liquid as he approached. "I thought you might need it."

Garrick groaned and stepped up his pace. "Come, Geoff. We have better things to do than deal with riffraff."

Geoff looked over his shoulder to catch Lauren's eye and pass her a quizzical look. She nodded assent so he caught up with Garrick.

Kyle handed Lauren the bottle of juice. "You look better today. How are you feeling?"

He had already departed for work when she'd awakened earlier, so she left a brief note thanking him for the considerate care. "I feel much improved, but ..."

Mara stared at her as if seeking words to question what Kyle meant. With the Thomases now several buildings ahead, Lauren didn't feel the need for restraint in expressing her friendliness with Kyle. After his kindness to her, Garrick was out of line being so critical. "I suppose I should be glad to have this juice. I think it—and you—pulled me through a bad time. I can't thank you enough."

"You're welcome to come back tonight," Kyle offered. "We could have a mutual appreciation party now that you've recovered."

Lauren laughed. "Thanks, but I need to spend more time with my mom." She put her arm around Mara's shoulder and pulled her close. Mara shrugged out of the embrace, looking confused.

"I see we're slipping early today," Kyle said, out of Mara's hearing.

"It's been a stressful morning. We took on Dr. Dickerson."

Kyle laughed. "Did you win?"

"I'd say no. Garrick termed it 'stonewalled'. I think that's pretty accurate. I don't understand why we're kept out of the loop on something that so much concerns us. I'm quite angry about the way we've been treated. Like we're children."

"Well … the people you're dealing with are trained to handle child-like folks. And I doubt that they're accustomed to demands for explaining unexpected deaths."

"I suppose you're right, but I don't have much more time to decide about Mother's future. I don't feel comfortable leaving her here at this point. On the other hand, I dislike upsetting her by a move if we can get a reasonable explanation and assurances in short order that she'll be protected."

"Understood, but they're probably in the dark too and don't want to admit it."

"Small comfort," Lauren groaned.

"Got to be on my way, but if you feel like having a social evening, I'll be around. You can stick to papaya juice, if you wish. There's plenty around here, and you can have it all." Kyle wrinkled his nose as he waved and turned to leave. "Or add some vodka to it," he called over his shoulder.

"Who is that nice young man?" Mara asked. "He looks familiar, but there's something about him …"

"Umm-humm."

"He seems to know you. Do you live here?"

"No, Mom. Time to take a nap."

❋ ❋ ❋

During the long afternoon after Mara was settled and asleep, Lauren took her bag of manuscripts to the mall. On the far side toward the sea, she found a pathway leading to the edge of the cliff and conveniently furnished with comfortable benches.

What more could one wish for, she sighed. A stunning view of the Caribbean, a warm, sunny day and privacy to engage in work you love. Better than being cooped up in a cluttered office. Maybe she'd plead insanity the next time she talked to Harry. She chuckled to herself. She doubted that disability insurance would cover relocation to Encantadora.

She had called Harry while waiting for Mara to fall asleep.

Mara couldn't understand why Lauren was calling and reminded her, "Burian doesn't have a phone. He's very old-fashioned."

Lauren shook her head. *You sound like you're in love with that creep.* She placed the call.

Harry had been sympathetic about her need for extending the stay at the island, even offered to send more manuscripts if she felt well enough to work. She didn't tell him the whole story, the part about the dead bodies, but instead emphasized her need to recover more fully before traveling. "I'm not making this up, Harry," she'd said. "I've been very ill."

"I know. I can tell by your voice. And your friend, whoever he is, claimed to be on the medical staff and sounded quite convincing. Take it easy. We'll survive without you, but take care of yourself. Anyone else and I'd think they were putting me on to stretch out a tropical vacation with some hot guy. You, I trust."

"And I appreciate what a decent guy you are, Harry. Truly, I look forward to getting back to the real world." *If you only knew!*

She pulled a manuscript randomly from the bag to begin reading and penciling edits. The plot was a whodunit and not exceptionally well written but engaging enough to survive with sufficient editing. Nothing to compare with the local activities, she thought, taking a swig from the bottle of papaya juice she'd brought along. Sans vodka.

Grateful for the privacy and silence save for the ocean's roar and lapping waves, Lauren progressed at a rate satisfactory to her expectations. After several hours, when she finally put the manuscript aside to finish reading during the evening hours, she decided to find Geoff. They needed to talk, without the parents present.

As she started to pack up the manuscripts, she heard whistling from not far off. She looked up to see Geoff approaching with a big smile on his pleasant face. "Hi," she called to him. "I was just planning to go looking for you."

"Well, and here I am. You must have a magic wand or something."

She liked his jovial manner, somewhat like his father's when he was in a better frame of mind than he'd displayed over much of the past couple of days. Considering the stress Garrick was under, however, she credited him with the right to be crusty about nearly everything.

"Here, let me move this bag. There's room for both of us." She placed the bag by her feet and patted the bench.

"Thank you," Geoff said, seating himself and leaning forward with his arms across his knees while he took in the view. "Magnificent," he breathed and straightened up. "It would appear our folks have been living quite well here."

"Under different circumstances, I would call it paradise."

"The one time I was here, I didn't take time to enjoy the scenery. I was mainly preoccupied with getting the old boy settled—he's not an easy case, you know."

Lauren laughed. "I've noticed. Neither is my mother, though I had felt comfortable with the care Mother has received. I'm not so sure now." She wondered how a caring offspring, as Geoff appeared to be, could leave his needy parent for such a long time without showing up occasionally. True, Garrick was difficult. Still …

"Do you buy the 'murder' bit?" Geoff asked.

"To a certain extent. I don't know that their middle-of-the-night accounts hold water, as imaginative as both are."

"Nor do I quite believe it, but with the rash of dead bodies turning up, I can see why they're unsettled, which is perhaps an understatement."

"Yes, and I witnessed one of the awful discoveries." Lauren shuddered at the dreadful memory. "Which was written off by the management as a transient from a boat."

Geoff reached over to squeeze her hand. "I can only imagine how awful it must have been for you and your mother."

"What are your thoughts on the hanged woman?" Lauren asked. "That one's hard to write off."

"I haven't a clue. These deaths—or murders—all seem orchestrated in different manners. Very strange."

Lauren sipped from the juice bottle. "I'd offer you some of this stuff, but you wouldn't want to catch my germs. Besides, it tastes like something concocted from the dishwasher after a heavy load."

Geoff laughed. "Perhaps you shouldn't drink it. You were quite ill, I understand."

"Yes, but I'm nearly back to normal. Just a little weak. This refreshing air helps."

"Would you care to have dinner with us this evening?" Geoff asked.

"Let me think about it, see how I feel later on, and how my mother feels. She gets pretty loosey-goosey late in the day, and this one has started off badly. Do you really have to leave tomorrow?"

"I do. A significant business deal awaits. Otherwise, I wouldn't hesitate to extend my stay."

"Do you plan to take your father back to England?"

"No way in hell—pardon me. The answer is 'no'. He would be unhappy. He'd make my wife's life miserable and mine unbearable with his criticism and controlling ways. What about your mother?"

"I'm undecided. I don't know where to take her, but if all these 'suicides' and 'accidents' aren't explained more thoroughly—and soon—I'll have no choice."

"I understand." He stood up. "I'd like to stay and keep you company, but I'd best be getting back before His Nibs gets into a rant."

Lauren picked up her bag and stood beside him. "I'll walk back with you, if you don't mind." She'd like to have time to question him about his father's problems, the nightmares, but he seemed in a hurry to leave.

"Your company is most pleasurable." He offered his arm.

Lauren laughed and slipped her arm into his. "What a gentleman. Too bad you're taken."

As they neared the mall, Lauren stumbled. She clung tightly to Geoff's arm. "Oh!"

Geoff helped her gain her footing and clasped his hand over hers clutching his arm. "What happened? Did you trip up on a pebble?"

"I-I don't know. I'm dizzy." She looked around for a place to sit but no benches were in sight. "Would you walk with me to Mom's apartment? I'm afraid I'm having a relapse." The nausea had returned. And the blackness bordering unconsciousness.

Chapter SIXTEEN

At Mara's apartment, Geoff insisted on sitting with Lauren until the dizziness passed. "What happened?" he asked.

"I'm afraid the crud has returned. I felt fine earlier, but this is how it started a couple of days ago. Dammit." She leaned back on the sofa and closed her eyes. "I'm sorry. You need to take care of matters with your father. I'll get over this."

"If you need me, I'll come back. Just call."

"Thank you, Geoff. I may return to Kyle's tonight if this keeps up. He's a trained medic and has been wonderfully helpful. Most of all, I don't want to disturb Mother if I'm up during the night."

"And the beast, to quote my old man, hasn't molested you?" Geoff seemed serious.

Lauren had to smile at Geoff's indoctrination by his father. "Not that I noticed, so I'll say no."

"I suppose dinner is out then. You won't feel like eating."

"That is a fact. Go ahead without me, and I'll make sure Mother has something to eat before I leave."

"She could join us," Geoff offered. "You may have your hands full, so I mean it. Call if you need help."

And he would have his hands more than full if he included Mara during the later hour, Lauren thought. "I will. Thanks again. And please don't mention to Garrick that I'm going back to Kyle's place."

"Who would dare?" Geoff laughed. "My ears couldn't take the battering. But be careful." With that, he left, quietly closing the door.

Lauren settled into the cushions, hoping the upheaval in her stomach would subside. She felt drained after the conversation with Geoff yet grateful for his concern. She truly hoped she wouldn't need to call on him for help.

But the queasiness didn't go away. She waited a little longer, then phoned the office and asked to have Kyle paged.

A few minutes later, he returned her call. "What's up?"

"It's back. The sickness. I just tossed the small amount of breakfast."

"What did you eat?"

"A little oatmeal and I've been carrying around the papaya juice you gave me."

"I gave—?"

"How could you forget? You said you wouldn't drink it. Maybe I'm allergic to the juice."

"Possibly, but not likely. Quit drinking it, at any rate," he said.

"Do you mind if I impose on you again tonight?"

"Of course not. I think that's a wise decision and certainly not an imposition."

"I don't know about wise. Desperate might be a better adjective. If I need someone to hold my head, I sure can't ask Mom for help."

"I won't question you about food right now, but I'll bring you something in case you feel better by evening. You didn't take my remark about vodka in the juice seriously, did you? That could be the problem."

Lauren almost laughed. "Of course not. I'm not stupid, uh … totally."

After ending the call, Lauren rested again on the sofa, hoping she could recover enough to take herself over to Kyle's. He had been so generous. She hated it that Garrick took such a negative attitude toward the man.

She had napped for what seemed only a few minutes when Mara awakened her.

"What are you doing here? Who are you? You have no right to sleep on my furniture." Mara's face was crimson, her hands shaking. "Get away and leave me alone. Why do you keep following me? Did Burian bring you here?"

Lauren sighed. *Here we go again.* "Mother, oh Mother, don't you recognize me?" Lauren knew how pointless it was to try reason. "I thought I'd fix something for your dinner."

"I'm too upset to eat. Just go away. I don't want you near my food."

"Let me make a phone call first." Lauren rang the office to ask for help. Mara had to have an evening meal, along with her late afternoon medications. She felt as if she should ask for medication for herself. She didn't know, however, what to ask for or even if the medics could dispense it without a doctor's examination and prescription. "Oh, hell," she said, after making the request for a nurse's aide and hanging up.

"Why are you still here?" Mara asked, her agitation increasing.

"I'm going but not until your nurse arrives."

"Nurse? I'm not sick. I will be if you people don't leave me alone."

Lauren felt less swimmy-headed but weak and didn't have the strength to argue. "I'm going." *But I'll be outside the door.*

She waited until Katie showed up. "She's in a state," Lauren said.

"I know. I'll fix her up."

As Lauren walked, once again, over to Kyle's cottage, she thought she should be grateful for Katie's help, but at the same time she felt guilty about giving in to making a call for more medication for her mother. She wished she could enjoy the prospect of an evening with Kyle, but all she wanted now was to go to bed—alone—to get over whatever was taking her down. She told herself that unless she recovered by morning she would indeed seek medical help at the infirmary.

❋ ❋ ❋

Kyle hadn't returned to his cottage by the time Lauren crawled into his bed, grateful that he was so generous as to share it—and relieved that he'd kept his distance. She was surprised that he didn't bring soup or something for her evening meal, but she didn't care. She didn't feel she could keep it down, anyway. In spite of her anxieties, she soon fell asleep.

When she awoke, after sleeping through most of the night with only a couple of sickness "episodes," the morning light shone around the edges of the drapes. This is getting to be a habit, she thought, and one I'd like to break. She could hear birdcalls through an open window. She lay still for a few minutes, gathering her senses.

When she sat up, the dizziness had disappeared. She hurried to wrap up in Kyle's robe before peeking into the living room. She expected to find him asleep on the sofa.

No sign of Kyle. "Silly me," she said. "He's back at work." She wondered that she hadn't heard him during the night, opening the door to look in on her or showering this morning.

She toasted a couple of slices of bread and spread them with butter and jelly. They went down well, to her great relief, guessing, praying, that she was finally over the nasty pip that had afflicted her. After she showered and dressed, she left the usual thank you note for Kyle and took off for Mara's apartment. With this reasonably early arrival, she hoped to be met with a friendlier reception than she'd fared the prior afternoon.

Lauren found Mara seated in the small front patio of her apartment building, scribbling on a pad of yellow lined paper. She looked up as Lauren approached.

"You bad girl," Mara admonished. "Where have you been? I had to go to breakfast with Garrick and his son and couldn't explain where you were. Garrick made some nasty insinuations."

"I'm sorry, Mom. I didn't feel well last evening and went elsewhere for medical care."

"Oh, dear. Are you all right? You don't have the flu, do you? You may have brought it from New York."

Lauren growled inwardly. She was pleased for Mara's lucidity this morning but annoyed by her paranoia, which wasn't exactly new, Lauren reminded herself. Her mother had always been a worrywart, always looking on the darkest side of whatever bothered her, and probably the reason she could write murder stories so realistically.

"I'm fine. I'm sure it was something I ate that didn't agree with me. What are you working on?"

Mara looked up and smiled. "I'm working on a new novel. I'm setting it on this island and using some of the unexplained murders for a tale that will get someone's attention."

Lauren's interest grew. God only knows what will come of this, she thought, but perhaps something can be extracted from reality to become fantasy, or vice-versa. In Mara's hours of clarity, she may have witnessed actions that would lead to the truth. "I'm excited for you, Mom. You go ahead and work. I'll get my manuscripts together and read alongside you."

Mara continued hastily writing. "You can take this to my agent when you return to New York. When are you leaving?"

"Soon, but I have a few days' leeway to make sure I've completely recovered."

"Maybe we'll have some real answers by then," Mara mumbled, "and I can take my story into a make-believe world."

Lauren retrieved her bag of manuscripts and settled on the chair beside her mother. After a few minutes, she asked, "Is Geoff still here then? I thought he was leaving early this morning."

Mara looked up, frowning at the interruption. "Yes, dear, but he changed his plans. He said he wants to stay a day or two longer to look for truth from the authorities. Now, let me go back to work."

"Yes, sorry." Lauren settled down to work, planning to seek out Geoff—and Garrick, if necessary—to see if they knew anything further. In a passing thought, she wondered where Kyle was. She could usually spot him around the mall in the mornings, attending to the other inmates. Then she slapped herself mentally for using that word, Garrick's word.

Chapter

SEVENTEEN

AS MORNING SLOWLY ADVANCED toward noon, Lauren felt pleased with herself to finally accomplish editing at least some of the work she'd brought along on the trip. She glanced over at Mara, seated beside her and still scribbling feverishly on the yellow pad.

"Don't you use your computer, Mom? You've always been so capable with it."

"Shhh, don't interrupt my thoughts. And, no, I seem to have too much trouble getting it to work the way it should."

Lauren rose from her chair and went upstairs to look for the computer. She knew Mara kept it on a table in a corner of the bedroom, unplugged. She plugged it in, turned it on and the computer whirred into action. She opened the word processing software and several databases. Nothing wrong that I can see, she told herself, followed by recognition that the problem wasn't with the computer but with its operator.

Unwilling to interfere with Mara's progress, Lauren returned to the patio but slipped on past her mother to walk back to Kyle's cottage. She didn't think he'd be there in the middle of the day, but she wanted to see if he'd found her note. *So unlike him not to keep in touch with me after a night together.*

She found the note where she had left it, apparently unread. Puzzled, she sat at the kitchen table, wondering if she should add to the note. She decided instead to place a call to the office to page him. But if she called from here, anyone recognizing Kyle's phone number, mainly the clerk Sheila, might read too much into it. *Oh, what the hell.* She picked up the phone and called the office.

"Main office, may I help you?"

Sure enough, Sheila answered. She who had observed their dissident group traipse in and out of Dickerson's office. So, no doubt, this call would be reported to the S.O.B. for whatever it was worth.

"I'd like to place a page for Kyle Vinson. It isn't urgent, but I would appreciate his return call." She gave Mara's number, deciding to wait there and hoping she'd still be welcome.

"I'm sorry, ma'am, but Kyle has gone over to George Town. He won't return for a coupl'a days."

"Oh … okay. Thank you." Lauren hastily replaced the phone in its cradle and held her head in her hands. What could this mean? So sudden. Why wouldn't he have told her when he knew she was at his cottage? *But then, I didn't see him last evening OR this morning. Has he been fired?*

This could not be good news. If he'd merely gone for supplies or to accompany a new "resident," wouldn't he have found time to tell her? Was he in trouble? Did the authorities believe her mother that Kyle was a murderer and arrested him? No, no, it couldn't be. He was too gentle to be a deranged killer. He'd shown no signs to her that he was anything but a thoughtful, decent person.

She surprised herself at becoming emotional over a man she had only known for a few days. A new and terrifying thought crept into her mind that Kyle himself had become the victim of a deranged killer. No matter what Garrick's attitude was, she had to discuss this with him. Had he gotten on his high horse again and demanded action, going over Dickerson's head to get Kyle fired? It might be possible, considering that his son was here, presumably of sound mind, and Garrick wanted to impress him. Garrick, who had worked for the British government, might have some pull. She didn't know in what capacity he'd served, but from his lofty manner she assumed it was at a respectable level.

Lauren raced through the house, barely thinking to close the front door after herself. At Garrick's, she burst in without knocking.

"What's wrong with you?" Garrick asked, surprise and annoyance written across his face. He and Geoff were seated at the table, playing a game of chess. "Lauren, this is most unlike you." He stood up and approached her. "Is your mother all right?"

"Yes, yes. This isn't about Mother. I have to ask, have you gone over Dickerson's head and complained to the George Town authorities about Kyle?" Her voice trembled, and she felt embarrassed by her show of emotion.

"What a marvelous idea. I wish I'd thought of it," Garrick chortled. "Son, why didn't you come up with that idea?"

"Did either of you?"

"And, madam, why are you so concerned? What is he to you?" He turned aside to Geoff, "As if I didn't know she's been sleeping over there with The Bastard."

Lauren felt herself coming apart. She was still weak and now, nearly in tears, she was giving way to rage. "Yes, I've been sleeping *at* Kyle's but not *with* him. He's been very much a gentleman. And now he's been sent—or taken—over to George Town."

"You protest too much. I believe this is the second or third time you've defended him to me so staunchly. If he's such a gentleman with so much temptation at his fingertips, he may be one of the loonies, too." He allowed himself another self-gratifying laugh. "What about you, son. Could you have been such a 'gentleman' under the circumstances?"

Geoff's face flushed. "Dad. Can't you see she's seriously upset? Why don't I go over to the office and make a polite inquiry about the reason for his absence. It's probably something simple, like a trip for supplies or medicines." Geoff headed for the door.

"I'll go with you," Lauren said.

Geoff shook his head. "I think it would be best for you to wait. Calm down, have a glass of water or some juice, and I'll be back in a few minutes."

"All right." She remembered then that she'd left Kyle's door unlocked. While he didn't normally keep his cottage locked, she was the last to leave, and if he were indeed to be away from the island for a couple of days, locking the door would be the responsible thing to do. She knew where he kept a key. "I'm going back to Kyle's for a minute. I need to lock his door."

"I'll do it while I'm out," Geoff said. "It's a simple doorknob lock like this one, isn't it?"

"Yes, but I need to pick up a key in case he didn't take one with him."

"Tell me where it is, and I'll fetch it."

Lauren told him where to find a key in the kitchen drawer below the microwave.

"You certainly know your way around his place," Garrick offered.

Lauren ignored him.

Geoff was on his way before Lauren had the wit to wonder how he knew where Kyle's cottage was, unless of course he'd been out on night patrol, accompanying his father on a spying mission. She felt faint and sat on a lounge chair to await his return. She had no desire to engage in conversation with Garrick, who was now pouring himself his afternoon toddy, the first, she hoped, as he could be difficult enough to deal with when he was sober.

Geoff returned a short while later, looking grim.

"What did you find out?" Lauren asked, glancing at Garrick, who had been uncustomarily quiet in his son's absence.

"The clerk who gave you the information admitted that she lied to you. He wasn't sent to George Town, but he has some personal time coming, so the people in the office assume he's merely taking time off. Under the circumstances, I didn't bother to lock his door."

"No, no, he wouldn't go without telling me," Lauren said. "They're covering up something."

Garrick spoke at last. "Why are you so sure? I'd hate to think that you do indeed have a thing going on with that man."

"I haven't seen him since yesterday afternoon." She decided to explain further. "It's unlike him, when I'm staying there, not to tell me if he won't be around. He said he'd bring food, and he didn't. There was no sign that he'd been home last night. I certainly didn't hear him."

"Maybe he's shacked up with someone else," Garrick offered.

"Ohhhh, you are so mean," Lauren cried, feeling her eyes start to water again.

"Dad, give her a break. You can see she's distressed. Please don't make it worse. You're letting your imagination take over your good sense."

"I'm sorry," Garrick apologized. "I suppose I have been out of line."

"What worries me most," Lauren said, "is that maybe he's become a victim like the others here. Maybe he discovered something."

"I seriously doubt it," Geoff said, "but then one can't be too certain in this environment, especially with the poor explanations we've received."

"I think we should go to Dickerson," Lauren said.

"That horse's ass?" Garrick shouted. "For all we know, he's the maniac behind the killings. I don't trust the man."

"We're very limited in who we can trust," Lauren said. "Who else can we turn to?"

Garrick snorted. "You know very well that scurvy man will tell us to mind our own business."

"I don't know about you, Garrick, but I feel this *is* my business. I'm right in the middle of it. From the first report by you and Mother to the missing host who has treated me so well."

Geoff intervened. "How are you feeling? Have you recovered from your illness?"

Lauren thought a minute. She'd been too wound up to think about herself. "I seem to feel okay." She almost laughed. "Maybe this has burned the bad bug out of me."

"I wouldn't count on it," Garrick offered.

Lauren looked at her watch. "Two o'clock! I haven't eaten anything today. I've been too upset to notice."

"There are sandwiches in the fridge," Geoff offered. "Okay, Dad?"

"Certainly. Please help yourself," he said as he poured another drink.

"Dad, don't you think it's a little early? You'll be pickled by four o'clock."

"That's my intent, dear boy."

Lauren opened the refrigerator and found a substantial supply of sandwiches. "Ham, egg salad, chicken, tuna, roast beef, what a selection," she said. "Are you expecting some sort of catastrophe?"

"More or less. We thought it wise to stock up," Garrick said. "One never knows when disaster will strike."

"Yes," Geoff muttered. "But with the type of disaster striking around here, one may not need a supply of food."

"What a pessimist you are, son, a regular chip-off-the-old-block, thus I can't deny your reasoning."

"You have quite a supply of papaya juice as well," Lauren noted. "Does everyone around here drink that stuff? I hate it." She looked over at Garrick, who stared into his drink.

"It's good for you," he offered.

"Not me. I think it was making me sick. Sicker, anyway."

Geoff stepped close to Lauren and lowered his voice. "I, for one, think we ought to clear off of this island. Pick up our folks, our bags and head out."

Garrick, whose hearing was obviously better than his son knew, jumped to his feet. "Yes, by God. Back to Merrie Olde England. I'll pack enough to get by. We can send for the rest."

"Hold on, Dad. We need to do this in a little more organized way. We don't have transportation lined up, for one thing."

"And I'm not sure how easily we can move my mother, if she's in one of her 'states'." Lauren paused. "But I'm willing to try."

"I'll go nose around the boat dock," Geoff volunteered, "find out when the next shuttle departs and see if we can book passage on the QT. Let's meet back here in an hour."

"Agreed," Lauren said, hurrying to the door.

Chapter

EIGHTEEN

Lauren rushed to Mara's apartment. She wanted to run but preferred to avoid drawing attention to herself. Nor did she wish to delay, praying that Mara would be awake and alert.

She found Mara seated at her usual post, crocheting doilies. She'd apparently given up whatever she'd been writing so furiously when Lauren left for Garrick's.

"Lauren, where have you been? I've been worried about you. With all these strange goings on and dead bodies everywhere, anything could happen."

"Mom, we're leaving. I'll pack a light bag for you and we'll go."

"Go?" Mara's face lit up. "Are you taking me home to Arizona?"

Her bright look at the prospect was heartbreaking to Lauren. "Maybe eventually. Right now, we're just plain leaving. Come with me. We need to pack."

Mara pushed herself up from her chair, stiffly. "I don't move so fast, you know, dear.

"I'll help you." Lauren assisted her to a firm stance. "Okay?"

"Yes, and I'll need to tidy myself in the bathroom." She beamed. "This is exciting."

Lauren located a small bag for Mara's clothing. She began opening drawers to check for essentials Mara would need during the transition. In a dresser drawer, she found the yellow pad Mara had been writing on so feverishly. Words were scrawled in barely legible handwriting, unlike Mara's practiced and elegant penmanship. Four pages were filled with descriptions of the scene on the mall. At the center of the activity on that dark night? Who else but Burian?

"Oh," Lauren groaned. This would scarcely stand up as evidence. She ripped the pages from the pad and buried them in her own suitcase, which had never been completely unpacked. She added a nightgown, slippers and a change of underwear to Mara's bag with just enough room for her light robe. They could always buy more clothing at the airport shops, though it shouldn't be necessary.

Wondering why Mara was taking so long, Lauren poked her head in the bathroom doorway. "Are you okay, Mom?"

Mara looked wild-eyed. "There's a strange woman in here, and she won't answer me." She pointed to her own reflection in the mirror.

"Oh, Mother dear, she won't harm you. She's just lost her voice. Come along."

"Who are you, and where are you trying to take me?"

Lauren chose not to answer, figuring anything she might say would cause further confusion. After depositing the bags beside the front door, she took Mara by the arm, clasped her mother's reluctant hand tightly in her own and led her to Garrick's cottage.

His door stood open. Lauren pulled Mara through the doorway and into the living room where they found Garrick sitting in his lounge chair, another drink in hand.

"Jesus, Garrick, aren't you ready to go?"

Geoff stepped from the bedroom, his face ashen. "You might as well hear it all. First off, shuttle service has been indefinitely canceled due to a weather alert."

"A hurricane? Oh, no, not now. What else can happen?"

Mara chimed in, "I think it would be exciting."

Garrick mumbled. "Not my choice for entertainment."

"Relax, everyone," Geoff said. "They're not predicting a hurricane but a serious tropical storm. Heavy rains and strong winds whipping the waves will make travel by small craft unsafe."

Lauren breathed in slight relief. "I guess that will slow us down for a day or so. If we stick together, we should be safe."

"Yes, but I wish I had a gun," Geoff said.

Garrick piped up. "I have one. Even have bullets for the bugger."

Geoff groaned. "Why wouldn't I suspect that?" He sat down heavily on the lounge chair facing Mara, now perched on the sofa.

She gazed around the room, staring past everyone. Looking to see if the woman in the mirror had followed her, Lauren suspected.

"But what will this do to your plans to return home," she asked, "let alone our escape plan?"

Geoff leaned forward, elbows on knees, face in hands. "I have no home, apparently."

Lauren frowned. "What do you mean?"

Geoff was silent.

"Go ahead, tell her, son. She's like family," Garrick growled.

Geoff started to speak, choked, covered his face again.

Lauren looked at Garrick. "What happened?"

"He'll have to tell you. Come on, Geoff. Lauren has had her share of marital disasters. She'll understand."

Geoff began again. "I got an email from Penny, my wife … "

"And …" Garrick prompted.

"She's divorcing me, and … "

"Worse," Garrick added.

"She says the baby isn't mine. He's the child of the man she's been cheating with." Geoff brushed his hand across his cheeks to wipe away a stray tear.

"I am so sorry," Lauren said. She stepped across the room to stand beside him, placed a consoling hand on his shoulder. "You seem like an awful nice guy to be treated so shabbily."

"He's well shut of her," Garrick interjected. "He just doesn't recognize it yet."

"I've had a bad marriage," Lauren said, "but notifying you by email with such wretched news beats anything I've had to deal with." She returned to the sofa, noting that Mara's gaze remained distracted. *Just as well. This is something that needn't concern her.*

"So, getting on with life," Garrick said, "I suggest we four hole up here. I have a king-size bed, and this sofa is a queen sleeper. I'm thinking, of course, safety in numbers."

"Yes," Geoff added, regaining control now of his emotions. "I don't think you ladies should be unprotected." He nodded toward Garrick, "And the old boy is armed—if dangerous, mainly to himself. Dad, how about you cut out the toddies now?"

Garrick gave him a sly look. "Actually, Mr. Prim, I cut them out a couple of hours ago. I've been drinking soda water with lime."

Geoff looked relieved. "Thanks for telling us. So how about you show me where you hide the pistol?"

"Wait," Lauren said, "I'm still concerned about Kyle. I'd like to check his cottage again to see if he's returned, or perhaps he left a message at Mother's by now. His disappearance without notice is unlike him."

"You don't have a cell phone number for him?" Geoff asked.

"I certainly could have used one a couple of times, but no I don't. And I'm not about to inquire again at the desk."

She could hear the rain beginning to splash off the eaves. A flash of lightning lit the room, closely followed by a deafening boom of thunder. Through the picture window, she could see the palms bending at unreal angles. "I'd better hurry." She started to leave.

Geoff restrained her. "No, no. It's too late to make a run in this weather. There is nothing we can do at this point but be grateful for our stash of sandwiches."

"You're right." Lauren sat down, sagged against the cushions. *Satan's found us at this tropical paradise.*

❋ ❋ ❋

By early evening, after what seemed an interminable afternoon of waiting with varying degrees of impatience, the foursome slumped in postures of defeat, exhausted by stress. The shrieking, high winds and the deluge of rain only added to the anxiety each felt from being trapped on a remote and treacherous island. The television carried nothing but storm warnings.

Lauren noted that her mother seemed focused inwardly on some unfathomable scenario playing out in her mind.

"Anyone up for a hand of bridge?" Garrick asked, at length.

Geoff moaned and Mara sighed.

"We can play three-handed and bid for the dummy," Garrick explained. "Or honeymoon bridge for two?" He waggled his eyebrows in Lauren's direction.

"I'm sure I couldn't concentrate," she responded.

"Nor could I," Geoff agreed.

"I may have to go back to the bottle for entertainment," Garrick said. "I'm tired of sitting here looking at four walls, windows streaming with water and grim-faced companions."

The lights flickered and died. "There goes the telly, too," Geoff said. "We're in for it and have no idea for how long. Even my cell phone is dead, so the wi-fi service is out, too."

A loud knock rattled the door. Geoff answered to find the tall Jamaican security guard, Samuel, standing beside a covered cart and protected by the overhanging roof. He wore a yellow slicker dripping rainwater. "Evening medicine," he said, looking around at the surprised faces. "And I've brought you a battery-powered lantern to get you through the evening. This storm looks like it's going to last awhile."

"Come in," Garrick said. "We're grateful for any diversion. Even pills. Especially pills, tonight."

"I'd mess up your floor, so I'll just hand these in, if you don't mind."

"Thank you," Geoff said, stepping forward to take the lantern. "Do you have any idea how long this is expected to last?"

"You never know with these storms, but you need to be prepared for getting through the night."

Lauren spoke up. "My mother, Mara Edwards, is here too, and we're planning to stay the night. I don't suppose you have her meds?"

Samuel looked at his chart. "As a matter of fact, I do. The front office consolidated the rounds. I don't usually have this duty, but one of the techs is off on leave, so the front office split up his load and shifted who handles what."

Lauren brightened, walked over to the doorway. "The man on leave, is that Kyle Vinson?"

"Sure is. Wish I were wherever he is." He located the pills for Garrick and Mara under the tarp covering the cart. "Take these now and these others at bedtime," he instructed as he consulted a printed sheet before handing over the plastic wrapped packets to Garrick. "It's all marked, so you can't get mixed up. No one will be around again this evening."

Lauren took Mara's packet. "Do you happen to know where Kyle is—on leave?"

"No, ma'am," Samuel replied. "We're not privy to personal information if a guy doesn't want to blab it. Did you try the office?"

"Earlier, yes." She let the subject drop at that point. No use getting someone too curious. After all, there was no real reason to worry about where Kyle might be. She tried to convince herself of that thought.

"Stay indoors and keep dry," Samuel said, aiming a meaningful look at Garrick and, over his shoulder, toward Mara.

"No doubt about that," Garrick assured him.

"Goodnight, all," Samuel waved his big hand as he trudged back into the storm.

❋ ❋ ❋

Following a meal of sandwiches and soft drinks, or whisky in Garrick's case, Lauren suggested that they retire early while granting that a good night's sleep was unlikely.

"But we'll save battery power," Geoff added. "We don't know what's coming next."

Chapter NINETEEN

DESPITE HOWLING WINDS AND heavy rain, the night ended without the disaster anticipated by three of the four housemates—or "inmates," as Garrick kept reminding them. Lauren had awakened several times to hear footsteps pacing outside Garrick's bedroom where she and Mara slept. He had insisted that "the ladies" sleep in a comfortable bed, while the "tough guys" could rough it on the sleeper sofa.

Lauren felt certain the footsteps were Geoff's. He was loaded down not only with concern for their combined welfare but also with the knowledge that his home life had been shattered. She wondered how much further stress the man suffered related to his business concerns. He had already postponed one important business meeting. What financial uncertainties must he be facing over his wife pulling out of the marriage? No one had mentioned the type of business he pursued. He seemed an intelligent, forthright person. She was sure that whatever line of work he engaged in, professional regard for Geoff would be high.

Her thoughts turned again to Kyle and his whereabouts. A chill crept over her when she considered the possibilities. Kyle had such a happy-go-lucky spirit, he could easily have stumbled headlong into the evil that pervaded the island. Could the occult science of Obeah, the Black Magic still practiced on islands such as St. Lucia, be at work here? *Nooo, I'm making too much of his disappearance.* He would no doubt turn up and laugh off her fears. If she were here when, and if, he returned.

Unable to sleep and with faint light creeping through the window, she decided to get up and make coffee—or tea—or both—for whomever chose one over the other, providing the power was back on. She looked up, relieved to see the overhead fan whirling. Things could be worse, she decided. But she needed something, anything, to keep busy—and quiet. No point in waking the others. Geoff's footsteps had ceased, and they all needed their rest for whatever actions lay ahead on this day. She only hoped there would be action. Worse would be having to sit still and fret about the right move. She'd done enough of that already.

Lauren slipped into the same clothing she'd worn the day before. She hadn't brought a change when fleeing from Mara's, so she had no choice. She only hoped her mother wouldn't become upset over wearing second-day clothing.

She crept quietly past the living room where the men slept and drew the kitchen's pocket door closed. After preparing both coffee and tea, she ate a bowl of cereal and wished she had a morning paper. She switched on the counter top tiny TV. Finding service resumed, she watched using closed captioning. Amid the sights of destruction shown throughout the Caribbean islands, at least no loss of life had been reported. Encantadora didn't rate a mention. Shuttle service was still suspended between the islands, however, and only those with airstrips would have transportation. Encantadora had no airstrip, she knew, but a heliport existed beyond the administration building.

She walked to the window and looked out on a scene that once again appeared calm, if wet. Large brown husks blown off the palm trees littered the ground along with fronds and other debris. She saw no flooding, no roofs or even tiles from roofs scattered around. The sky looked all sparkly and sunshiny like nothing bad happened over night. If she could only believe that, more concerned with human risks than with the landscape. She wouldn't be surprised to hear that more bodies had turned up on Encantadora.

As she finished her second cup of coffee, sounds of stirring came from the living room. "There's one, at least," she said, and began to place cereal bowls around the table.

Geoff slid the door open. He looked exhausted, his blond hair uncombed, purplish wells under his eyes. "Good morning," he said, helping himself to a cup of coffee.

"Good morning to you, too." She watched as he opened a sugar packet and sprinkled the contents into his coffee. "What's this? You're not a tea drinker? Are you really a Brit or an imposter?"

"Sometimes I drink tea. I prefer coffee in the morning to get my motor running." He yawned.

"I heard you up during the night. I know you're worried."

"More than worried. If I can't get out of here today, I'll go nuts myself."

"You'll have a lot of company." Lauren noted his pained expression and instantly regretted popping out a facetious remark when the man was under heavy stress. Still, she hoped that by keeping their conversation light, some of his tension would ease.

The doorbell's ring startled the pair.

"Garrick has a doorbell?" Lauren asked. "I've never heard one in my entire time on this island. Everyone knocks."

"They have doorbells, I've noticed. If no one uses them, I suppose they prefer to bark their knuckles," Geoff said. "It's a guy thing."

Lauren moved to answer the door. When she opened it, she let out a shriek. "Kyle. Where did you come from?"

"Heaven, Sweet Thing. Hadn't you guessed?" He chucked her under the chin as he walked past her to introduce himself to Geoff. "I heard you were here to visit your father. Welcome. I'm sure he's pleased."

"Well …" Geoff began. "Tell me, have you been off the island? We were worried about you."

Kyle's jaw tightened, then relaxed. "I had an errand for Dickerson. I've been over at George Town."

"Tell me, man, are the shuttles running then?"

"No, I had to beg a ride on a helicopter to get back here."

"Must have been expensive," Geoff said.

"Expense account, company business." Kyle turned to Lauren with a smile. "I heard you were asking about me."

Lauren had stayed mute during the dialogue between the two men but now opened up. "Of course, I was worried to death. It's unlike you to go away and not tell your houseguest—especially after you promised to bring her food. I entertained dark thoughts that you'd become another victim."

Kyle grinned. "I am deeply flattered, and I apologize for not letting you know. This was a hurry-up mission orchestrated by Dr. Mastermind, and I had no time to tell you. I figured you wouldn't starve with canned soup in the cupboard."

"I was too upset to look for food. You have to admit, Kyle, that this island is spooky with an untold number of deaths and no credible explanations for the causes."

She thought Kyle looked uncomfortable, but then why shouldn't he? He'd caused her a great deal of worry. If he knew how much, he'd probably be pleased. She didn't care if she sounded like a shrew, though she guessed it was time to ease off.

"So, was the storm as bad where you were?" she asked. "It was quite heavy here."

"Grand Cayman was affected pretty much the same as here but still no reports of fatalities, that we know of."

"And that's saying a mouthful ..." Garrick interrupted, shuffling into the room in bare feet.

All turned toward him, surprised.

He continued "... considering we're dropping like flies around here in the good weather." He poured himself a cup of tea before lunging onto a chair at the kitchen table. "What are you doing out so early? And where exactly have you been?"

"Why don't you sit down and join us, Kyle?" Geoff offered in an obvious attempt to mollify his father's surliness.

"I wish I could," Kyle said, "but I only came by with the morning's meds. After the extra duty the others had yesterday, I'm making up for it today. I understand your mother is with you, Lauren, so here's her morning packet. Are you okay with giving them to her?"

"Sure. I haven't seen her since I got up, but I'm sure she'll be along pretty soon." It occurred to Lauren that the staff was pretty loose with administering pills to residents. How could Samuel last night and now Kyle today trust outsiders, even family members, to see that their loved ones were given the proper doses? Especially with someone like Garrick who already had a reputation for ducking his meds.

Geoff spoke up. "We four are planning to leave the island. You may as well know, but we were delayed by the lack of shuttle service."

Kyle looked surprised. "You're serious about leaving?"

Garrick replied. "We've had enough of this horseshit from Dickerson. Either we get some straight facts about what's going on or we clear out. In fact, I'd prefer to clear out, regardless of Stonewall Dickerson."

"I see, but I'd better report your plans to him, if you haven't. Maybe he'll come through with an explanation."

"I have to leave, regardless," Geoff said, "and I feel strongly that I should take my father with me."

Lauren spoke up, "I need to do the same with my mother. I can't feel comfortable leaving her alone when I live so far away."

"But she's not alone," Kyle argued. "Each and every one of us here has her interests up front. Trust me, Lauren. She's been well cared for, and that will continue."

"I'd like to believe you, Kyle, but after your sudden, overnight disappearance, how can I know it won't happen again. And how can I believe there isn't a psychopath running around this island?"

"Come now, Lauren. You know better. As Dickerson told you, with this population we experience natural deaths all the time. And a few who are suicides, but that goes with the territory, too."

"Indeed," Garrick grumped. "We still need to hear the outcome of our report direct from the horse's ass."

Kyle glanced at him and quickly buried his exasperation. He turned to Lauren. "I haven't even asked how you're feeling. Are you okay now?"

"I seem to be back to normal, thanks."

"Kind of a coincidence," Garrick offered, "that she recovered as soon as you left."

"Garrick." Lauren couldn't contain her annoyance. "Please. Kyle is our friend. We need him on our side." She turned to Kyle. "Can you help us book transportation if we decide to go through with our plan? Geoff, most certainly, needs to leave, and I will too, very soon. Whether Garrick and Mother accompany us remains the big question."

"I will help as much as I can," Kyle offered, "but as an employee it's not my place to encourage you to remove your loved ones from a location where they are well treated."

"I understand. Thank you for being my friend. You've already helped me through a most unpleasant illness." She looked over at Garrick, whose expression of skepticism left no doubt about his attitude—had anyone entertained a doubt prior to this.

"Good morning, everyone," Mara trilled as she stepped lightly into the room and seated herself at the table. "What is this about removing our loved ones? Who is going anywhere?"

Lauren sighed. *How are we to explain this?* "Mom, Kyle dropped off your meds and is just leaving. Thank you, Kyle. Can we talk later?"

"Sure. Why don't you meet me on the mall after lunch?"

"If we're in town," Garrick said.

"I'll walk with you," Geoff said. "I'm going over to the dock to see what to expect of the shuttle runs."

Chapter TWENTY

"Now, what?" Garrick asked, his continuing irritation ill-concealed. "Don't tell me we're going to stick it out on this godforsaken lump of limestone and sand. You and Geoff go your merry ways, while Mara and I play Dodge 'Em with criminals."

"Really, Garrick?" Lauren asked, thinking to change the subject. "I didn't know you were familiar with computer games."

Garrick looked contrite. "I use the computer for a few things other than writing. I play a little Solitaire."

Lauren laughed. "I should have guessed that you're a games player."

"So you're going to run off and leave the old people. Right?"

"We have much to discuss. We'll certainly not leave you here if we think you're in danger."

Geoff entered the cottage quietly following his trip to the dock. His expression signaled that the effort had not gone well. "Far too much wave activity to run the shuttles. Deep swells could capsize the boats."

"Did you inquire about a helicopter?" Garrick asked.

"I did, but they're in high demand in view of the medical evacuations throughout the islands."

"One wonders how your friend," Garrick nodded toward Lauren, "managed to commandeer one."

Lauren sighed, resigned to Garrick's negative attitude. She might feel the same way were she in his situation. "I doubt that it was 'commandeered'. He claimed his trip was for Dickerson. I'm assuming he was returning with emergency medical supplies."

"Possibly, though he didn't state as much," Garrick said. "He could have been picking up bimbos for his boss."

"Da-a-a-d, let it go, will you?" Geoff pleaded. He turned to Lauren. "What do you actually know about this Kyle? Is he to be trusted?"

"From all I can tell, he's a straight arrow."

"Aside from trying to poison you with papaya juice," Garrick intervened.

Lauren's eyebrows shot up. "What do you mean? You think I was poisoned?"

"The man handed me the juice to give to you, didn't he? Why wouldn't he give it to you himself if nothing were wrong with it. And think about your symptoms."

"True, I recovered after I quit drinking the juice," Lauren said. "Oh, my God. Do you really believe he poisoned me?" She held her head. "No, no, I can't believe that. What would have been his motive?"

"Do psychopaths need motives?" Garrick asked.

"I've seen no indication that he's anything but a kind person," Lauren protested. "He certainly didn't try to take advantage of me while he gave me shelter."

"I have to agree with Lauren, Dad. What evidence do you have that Kyle is anything but honest? Have you been talking to your pal Phelan again?"

"Cheap shot, son. I'm taking the *prima facie* evidence of the juice making Lauren ill. Come to think of it, Phelan hasn't been around for a while," he laughed. "Chalk it up to your presence." He turned to Mara. "How about you? Have you been in touch with Burian recently?"

"Who?" Mara looked startled.

"Your alter ego. The villain of your stories."

"Oh," Mara giggled. "I see him now and then, but the last time I spoke with him he said he's been busy."

Lauren took a deep breath, trusting that Burian would stay busy—elsewhere.

Garrick continued, "Must be all the commotion from P.I.'s driving him out."

"P.I.'s? You mean private investigators?" Mara asked.

"No, I mean Positive Influences. Your daughter and my son. We've had quite a lot of commotion since they arrived."

"Thanks, Dad. We'll be more than happy to depart, eh, Lauren?"

"You bet. I'm ready to return to Dullsville now, though I've never in my life thought I'd view the Big Apple as dull."

"So, providing the shuttle service is up and running by tomorrow, say, when do you expect us to clear out?" Garrick asked.

"Tomorrow couldn't be too soon," Lauren answered. "But first, we need to reconsider taking our folks out of here."

"And if they want to go," Geoff said.

Garrick choked. "Is there any question, in my case?"

"Mom, how about you? Would you feel safer and more comfortable in New York?"

"New York? No. I want to go home to Arizona. If I can't go there, I'll stay here and take my chances."

"Certainly," Garrick suggested, "you can have more picnics with your chums at The Grotto."

"Garrick," Lauren growled, "don't make it worse than it is."

"Can it get any worse?" he asked.

Geoff drummed his fingers on the table. "We'll all be crackers if we don't get out of here fast. And I mean today."

"We're trapped essentially," Lauren said. "But at least we can contact the outside world by cell phone or internet. It's not as if we couldn't call for help."

"Who couldn't possibly get here in time," Garrick offered, "to prevent us from being tossed over the cliff."

Lauren heaved another sigh. "We have to trust someone, and Kyle seems our only ally, in spite of what you think. If the juice was poisoned, it was no doubt an accident. Sitting on the shelf too long, or something."

"But more than once?" Garrick asked.

"Probably from the same container," Lauren conceded. *But I suppose that is unlikely. I didn't see any open containers.*

Geoff seated himself at Garrick's computer, which he'd rolled on a stand into the kitchen. He began typing.

After a few minutes, Garrick asked, "Anything new from 'home'?"

"Nothing. I'm just letting the office know of the delay so my secretary can make calls and cancel appointments for another day or so."

"What type of work are you engaged in, Geoff?" Lauren asked.

"I'm a banker, real estate specialist." He continued to type without looking up.

Garrick laughed. "I'll bet you wouldn't put a high price on this place."

"Not funny, Dad." He continued to type. "Hah! Our head man just authorized helicopter service to get me out of here."

"Us," Garrick added. "Provided they can find one that isn't in service to the government at the moment."

"Provided that," Geoff agreed.

Mara pulled her crochet needle and thread from a pocket and hummed happily to herself after moving to a corner of the living room, near a window and away from all the noise. Lauren thought she seemed the only happy party present.

"Have you heard anything further from Penelope?" Garrick asked Geoff.

"Not a word. At least, she hasn't cleaned out my, our, bank account, but she did make a sizable withdrawal from savings."

"Who is this bugger she's taken off with? Anyone you know?" Garrick asked.

"He belongs to our club. Has a lot of money and a yacht. I always liked him, before this."

"I guess she did, too."

"I don't know how long this has been going on." Geoff shut down the computer and turned to face them. "Apparently for some time. I could deal with losing Penny," he said. "You had her pretty well pegged, Dad. She can be a bitch. But finding out this baby on the way isn't even mine, that is a real blow to the gut."

"Maybe she lied about him not being yours so you wouldn't go after custody," Lauren said.

"I hadn't thought of that. It wouldn't be beneath her. Hell! This is pure hell."

"I'm sure it is, Geoff," Garrick sympathized. "But you're strong. You'll get over it."

"I suppose. But when I get home, I'm going to insist on a DNA test for the baby after he's born. If I find out he's mine, I'll go to court if I must to demand custody. And you can be damned sure that I'll fight for custody of my son Jeffie at the same time. We know he's mine because he looks like Dad."

Garrick beamed. "Must be a handsome little fellow. Good thinking, son. Go for it."

"Yes," Lauren agreed. "Smart move."

"Has she had the decency to move out of your home?" Garrick asked.

"She said she's in the process." Geoff hung his head. "It will be big and lonely without my family."

Garrick leered. "Son, you won't be alone. You'll have me."

Lauren tried not to read Geoff's expression.

"Sure, Dad." He stood up and looked around. "The first move remains to be getting out of here. I'm going over to dicker with Dickerson and see what I can do. After all, he got Kyle back in spite of the limited—or nonexistent—service."

"Are you going to mention taking our families with us when we go?" Lauren asked.

"I may as well get it out in the open. Do you care to go with me?"

"Yes, I believe I should."

"I'll go, too," Garrick offered.

"No, Dad. Please. You'll lose your temper and stir things up when we need his cooperation."

"I suppose you're right. I'll stay here and keep an eye on Miss Marple. We can play one of our little 'guess who I am today' games."

Lauren laughed. Geoff looked quizzical. "I'll explain on the way over to Dickerson's," she told him.

❋ ❋ ❋

At the front desk, Sheila eyed Lauren suspiciously.

Lauren returned her look. *Do I detect a hint of jealousy? After all, Kyle is a good-looking, fun-loving guy. Maybe he's shining us all on. The women, anyway.*

"May we speak with Dr. Dickerson," Geoff asked the clerk.

Lauren appreciated his polite, business manner. So unlike his father, whose magma too often spewed from that old volcano.

Sheila rang Dickerson's office. "He said just a minute. Have a seat, please."

The two remained standing. "Have you heard anything during the past hour about the shuttle service," Geoff asked her.

"Nothing new. Maybe Dr. D has an update."

Ten minutes later, Dickerson's door opened, and Kyle exited. He looked surprised when he saw the pair. Sheila hadn't announced their names when she buzzed in to tell Dickerson that visitors were waiting. She just told him "a coupl'a people."

Lauren answered his questioning look. "We're here to talk about taking our families home."

Kyle frowned. "I'm sorry to hear that. I'd hoped you would reconsider after my pep talk."

"Incidentally," Geoff said, "my company has authorized leaving by helicopter, once one becomes available."

"Good for you," Kyle said, though apparently not cheered by the news. He looked at Lauren. "I suppose you'll leave with him?"

"I'm not sure. I hope so, if it can be worked out."

"I'll admit that I'm disappointed. I have enjoyed your company."

"I'll bet, watching me toss my cookies." Then she remembered the papaya juice. "I need to talk to you about that."

Dickerson appeared in his doorway.

"Later," Lauren added, nodding to Kyle.

She and Geoff were ushered into Dickerson's office with his usual courtesy. Whether faked or real, he puts on a good show, she thought.

Geoff began, once they were seated. "We have several issues."

"You want to remove your parents from our care," Dickerson offered.

"You know already?"

"Yes. Kyle and I discussed the matter a few minutes ago."

Lauren interrupted. "Garrick is anxious to go. I'm not so certain about my mother, but I am deeply concerned about her safety. There have been too many unexplained deaths. And we have yet to hear whether the man our parents described has turned up."

"I understand your concern," Dickerson said in a placating manner. "These matters are never easy to unravel—"

"When they're told by lunatics," Geoff interrupted. Apparently realizing that he sounded like his father, he backed down. "I'm sorry, but I'm running out of time here. I've already overstayed the days allotted for being away from my business concerns. Please explain exactly what steps are being taken to identify the man Dad and Mara reported."

"First, sir, we have yet to locate a body. I've already told you that we have no verification from the staff that anything unusual occurred that night. It, therefore, has not been my highest priority."

"So you think they fantasized the whole scene? From two different vantage points at the same time?"

"It's not a great stretch and stranger things happen around here. You surely understand what I mean. It's possible that one created the scene and convinced the other. Both have highly developed imaginations."

"True enough." Geoff's shoulders returned to slumped dejection. "I still plan to take my father back to England with me. He's been here long enough."

"I see," Dickerson said. "And you, Ms. Hale?"

"I would like to have my mother remain, but only if you can guarantee her safety."

Dickerson paused before he spoke. "I'm sure you know there can be no guarantees without moving your mother to a locked ward. Is that what you want?"

Lauren caught her breath. "Oh, Lord, no. She'd die in such confinement."

"And what would be your arrangements in New York?"

"It was bad before I brought her here. I would have to find a satisfactory assisted living facility. Sadly, she has seemed contented at your facility until recent events."

"You would not want me to make up answers, would you?" Dickerson asked. "Do you not think, perhaps, that you may be stirring the pot by buying into their fantasies?"

Lauren's frustration broke through. She started to rise. Geoff placed his hand on her wrist, and she settled back in her chair. "Do you think I'm causing her to be frightened? Is that what you're saying?"

Dickerson nodded. "It is quite likely."

"I'm sorry, but I'm pretty uptight about all this, plus I've been ill and now it seems impossible to get off the island."

"Yes, I understand. The decision is yours, of course. I recommend that you leave her with us, and it is not for our financial gain. I truly believe she has the best life a person in her condition can expect. Furthermore, the best the families of persons in her condition can expect."

"I suppose you're right. I'll make my decision between now and tomorrow. I'd like to try to talk to her about it in the morning when she's clearer headed."

"Of course. And you, sir, when do you propose to depart?"

"As soon as transportation is available. How did you manage to get Kyle over here so quickly from George Town?"

"We had priority due to medical needs. I'll give you the phone number of the helicopter service if you so desire."

"Please. And we'll need to settle up my father's account before we depart."

"You do realize there's a hefty penalty if the contract is broken for any reason other than death."

"I do."

"So be it, then. I'll have the paperwork prepared and delivered to his cottage. I'm sorry to lose your father. He's been a challenge at times but always a man I respect for his forthright spirit."

Chapter

TWENTY-ONE

Lauren stopped at Mara's apartment, after telling Geoff politely that she wanted to think through what plans she should make, without interruption.

"I understand," he said. "It's difficult when you have too much advice. I'll see you later."

She felt hopelessly uncertain about whether it was wise to leave Mara on the island. Dickerson could be right. The sighting her mother and Garrick claimed could be a work of the imagination by one or the other—or both.

She poked around the rooms, looking to see if she'd missed anything that might be needed. She found nothing necessary to add, to stuff into the already overloaded bags, and she prepared to leave when Kyle showed up at the bedroom door.

"Hey," he said.

"Hey, yourself. You do have a way of surprising people."

"I hope I didn't frighten you. The front door was ajar."

"No, no. I'm glad to see you." She'd been startled, of course. Knowing Kyle was opposed to her removing Mara from the island, she wanted to explore the possibilities of leaving her here. He knew his way around the whole setup of the clinic by now, and she still believed him to be honest.

"How did it go with Dickerson?" he asked.

"How would you expect? He was polite but adamant in his belief that the parents made the whole thing up."

"It is possible," Kyle agreed, "though they both seemed highly determined in their reports and quite clear, considering … "

"Considering their memory lapses. Mother's is far worse than Garrick's."

"They could be feeding off one another's imaginations. One recalls details, sets the scene. The other studies the scene and telegraphs more details back to the other. The lack of a body does make it a stumper, you must admit."

"No doubt about it," Lauren agreed. "But here's the question. If someone went so far as to kill another person, wouldn't it be reasonable to assume the killer would find it expedient to dispose of the body? And that by now someone would be reported as missing?"

"Presumably, though this tiny island has been thoroughly searched. I headed up a fair share of it myself. No one is missing from among the staff or the residents."

"What about the body in The Grotto? We haven't heard that he has been identified, and I'm not sure I buy the idea that he was a stranger who jumped or was dumped from a boat. Could he have been a visitor, someone's family member?" Stumbling onto that idea didn't bring her comfort.

"Highly unlikely. Visitors check in and out at the office. No one merely walks on without being processed. You saw that yourself."

"What about picnickers from boats?" Lauren asked. "They surely aren't 'processed'."

"Well … true. But I doubt that any of them would have been on the mall at night."

"Possibly up here to steal?"

"C'mon. It's true this island had a reputation for pirates in the past, but … "

"Who's going to raid a lunatic asylum?"

"For drugs, possibly, but we have protective measures in place. You've met Samuel. He heads up the island's guard service, and he was present that night after the commotion."

"Did anyone check the surveillance tape? Surely, one is in place at a facility like this."

"Of course. I took care of that myself. I couldn't find a thing."

Lauren didn't want to bring up her mother's continued insistence that the murderer was Kyle. She herself didn't believe it. After all, the male staff members all dressed in shorts most of the time. Of course, they couldn't all be described so colorfully as Mara had depicted Kyle's legs.

"Kyle, let me ask you something."

"Sure, go ahead."

Lauren smiled. "When you gave me the papaya juice, did you add anything to it?" Lauren expected him to say no, but she wanted to observe his reaction.

"Like what? Did it taste funny?"

"I wouldn't say 'funny'. It tasted like shit, and I have no idea what papaya juice is supposed to taste like."

"It's sweet and fruity, of course. It has a distinct musky flavor, but I wouldn't describe it as 'shit'. I'm not overly fond of the stuff myself, but it is supposed to have some health benefits, like to aid digestion, possibly to prevent colon cancer or heart disease. Half a dozen other things. And what do you mean that I gave it to you?"

"Garrick told me you had left it for me. I thought perhaps it was spoiled or tainted from being old and you weren't aware of it. I did recover after I stopped drinking the stuff."

"Huh? I did not leave it for you, Lauren. The old coot must have cooked up that story himself to make me look bad."

"I can't believe he'd do such a thing. I realize he's not fond of you, but how could he come up with such a monstrous plan, making me the victim?"

"Who knows what goes through the man's mind? Do you have any of the juice remaining?"

"There's a small amount in your refrigerator. Would you take a look at it?"

"Better than that, I'll take it over to the lab and have it tested."

"Great idea. How soon will you know?"

"I'll get right on it, though it might be tomorrow before we know the result. I'm on rounds at the moment, but I'll swing by, pick it up and drop it off. I'll ask the lab tech how long it will take for the analysis."

"Thanks, Kyle. I owe you big time for this and for your other kindnesses."

"Nah. Your sweet presence is all the thanks I need. See you later."

After he left, Lauren sat down to calm herself. What on could Garrick be thinking to try such a stunt? She'd certainly been miserable, and if he were the one who had made her ill, then she had no business leaving her mother at his cottage. True, he had mental problems, but he'd seemed coherent when she'd been with him. Surely, Kyle would find that the juice was not intentionally tainted, that the problem resulted from the can sitting too long on the shelf.

What to do about Mara was still the big question. Leave her here, alone, without even Garrick to care about her after he left with Geoff? Or move her to New York where she'd be miserable again? If she were to take Mara with her, she needed to make arrangements right away. That would be no small job, but she could hire someone to ship the remainder of Mara's clothing, books and personal items, as Garrick planned for his belongings. She'd packed enough now for her to get by for at least a week. Then, too, the cancellation fee needed to be handled. Lauren had in mind, from reading the original contract, that the sum was five thousand dollars. Worth it, she thought, if it could save her mother's life. Living here wasn't cheap, so she doubted that a New York facility would cost more and possibly less. Money wasn't the problem.

She wanted to discuss the possibilities further with Geoff before she reached a decision.

Wouldn't it be great if they could find a facility where both parents could live close to one another, happily ever after? *Yeah, in your dreams.* Geoff would probably be happy to lodge Garrick in New York, though convincing Garrick would be another matter.

She stirred up a cup of instant coffee and heated it in the microwave. The coffee wasn't half bad—or good—but gave her something to do while she tried to sort out the future. She checked her wristwatch. Two-thirty, and she hadn't had lunch, nor had Mara unless Garrick pulled out another of his endless supply of sandwiches.

Lauren hurried to Garrick's cottage. She found him snoozing noisily in his patio. Mara was asleep on the living room sofa. *All's well—at least quiet.* Geoff was nowhere in sight. She figured he was back down hanging around the boat dock.

She needed something to eat and thought maybe peanut butter and jelly would do the job. She was wary now of Garrick's supply of sandwiches. She didn't know how long he'd kept them in the refrigerator. They hadn't appeared to be moldy, which in this humid climate didn't take long to develop. No one seemed to have become sick from eating the sandwiches.

She poked around in Garrick's kitchenette cupboard until she found the peanut butter. To reach it, she had to pull out a container of syrup. Ipecac, she read. *I wonder what he uses that for?* She'd heard of it but never known anyone to use it. Reading the label, she found it to be an emetic useful for inducing vomiting in the event of poisoning.

Could Garrick have had someone get this for him as a possible way to help her recover from the presumed poisoning? How sweet, she thought, considering he may be the accidental poisoner. He really is an old softie. She returned it to the shelf, not quite so hungry after reading the label. She settled for a couple of crackers she found on the counter.

Chapter

— TWENTY-TWO —

Faced with choices, none of them good, Lauren couldn't relax. While Garrick and Mara napped and Geoff frantically searched for a means to escape the island, Lauren paced about the small living room. Decision-making had never been difficult for her, but now? How could she in good conscience leave her mother in this questionable environment?

She couldn't. Mara would have to go with her as soon as Geoff rounded up transportation. Whatever would come next must simply be worked out once she returned to New York. As she reached the open door, she spotted Geoff approaching, far along the mall. He might as well know her plan—and she needed to know what he'd discovered.

Geoff waved when he saw her and stepped faster. She rushed out to meet him, hoping to talk far enough away from the cottage to avoid disturbing Garrick's nap.

"Good news, more or less," he called, breathless, his face dripping sweat. As they met along the walkway, he stopped and took a moment to pull up his loose-fitting T-shirt to wipe his brow. "The shuttles will begin running tomorrow morning, early."

"Thank God." Lauren couldn't contain her relief. "We can leave this blighted place. Only one more night of living hell."

Geoff laughed. "I guess you aren't having a good time?"

"I can honestly say I've never known worse. Even a nasty divorce couldn't top this for sick entertainment." She was instantly sorry she'd made the remark, seeing Geoff's downcast look, no doubt reminded of what lay ahead when he returned to England.

Geoff looked up, appeared to catch the sympathy in her eyes, and switched back into high gear. "I took the liberty of booking all four of us aboard. I wasn't sure about your mother but thought it best to include her. Easier to cancel than to add later."

"You gave up on taking the helicopter, I assume."

"I could never get a firm commitment and with the shuttle available tomorrow, yes, I gave up."

"I have made up my mind that Mother is to go with us. What time do we depart?"

"We need to be at the dock by five a.m. for processing, though the shuttle isn't scheduled to leave until six-thirty."

"I can deal with that. I probably won't sleep tonight, anyway."

"Doubtful that either of us will. Getting the parents up and on the move from their drugged dreams will probably be the biggest challenge."

"We could ask that their pills be held back or lightened at bedtime," Lauren suggested.

"I don't think so. Do you want to spend a night hearing the struggles with Phelan and Burian? Heaven help us if they ever meet."

"Right," Lauren agreed. "What resourceful minds our folks have. I wish Mom had stuck to children's stories."

Geoff laughed. "Then we'd probably get to witness Phelan gobbling up Little Red Riding Hood or raping Cinderella."

Lauren groaned. "I feel so hopeless about dealing with this whole situation. Bringing my mother here seemed a good solution at the time."

"In my case," Geoff said, "it was the *only* solution, I believed. I thought Dad merely needed to dry out. I didn't know he'd started publishing as Phelan Powell several years earlier. I knew he'd begun drinking heavily but assuming his villain's alter ego was what finally drove him over the top. I should never have been so inattentive."

"I think you're too hard on yourself, Geoff. Your father is a strong-willed man. I doubt that you or anyone could have anticipated the situation becoming such a crisis. At least, that's what I've gathered from talking to him."

"He blames me for sticking him here and leaving him to rot, as he likes to describe it. I have to admit to a certain amount of truth in that view. I've been so wrapped up in my career and family—" He choked and turned away.

Lauren placed her hand on his arm. "You have a load on you right now, Geoff. If you ever need a friend, you'll know where to find me."

Geoff relaxed. "Our worlds may be an ocean apart, but I do have occasions when I travel to New York, so you may regret those words when I come whining on your doorstep."

Lauren laughed and removed her hand after a friendly pat. "I'll look forward to seeing you again. Right now, I'm going over for one last sweep through Mom's apartment to see if I missed anything essential. Oh, and who did you speak with about packing up and shipping Garrick's belongings after we leave?"

"I arranged it through Sheila in the office. Don't forget the medications. You'll need a supply and prescriptions."

"I'm glad you reminded me. I need to go over there anyway to cancel the contract and pay the fee. See you later."

Geoff waved as he turned toward Garrick's cottage. "Good luck," he called over his shoulder.

Lauren started toward Mara's apartment, then changed her mind and went to the office first. She was glad she'd carried her purse to Garrick's so she wouldn't have to take time to retrieve it at Mara's. She had thought to bring along on this trip Mara's power of attorney for health purposes and for accessing her bank account.

The afternoon was moving on, which concerned Lauren. She didn't wish to risk arriving at the office after the day staff had closed up. She wasn't sure how much authority the evening crew would have for closing an account. Might as well get the business over with, she knew it wouldn't be pleasant. She didn't particularly like Sheila and sensed that the feeling was mutual. And Dickerson, the control freak, was another matter altogether. She dreaded the possibility of running into him.

Lauren stepped into the office and announced her needs to Sheila. She'd decided ahead of time to take control of the situation and not be bullied by the woman.

Sheila responded pleasantly, a welcome surprise, and the paperwork proceeded more smoothly than Lauren had anticipated. Without Sheila's earlier smug looks and now told by her that Dickerson was tending to business in the infirmary, Lauren relaxed a little. He might call them back over later, Sheila said, but by then everything would be in place. There was no way he could talk Lauren out of her decision.

"One thing more," she asked Sheila, "could you have the same people pack up Mother's belongings and ship them to me when they handle Garrick Thomas's?"

"Sure. Give me a credit card and delivery address, and we'll take care of it. You might not receive them for a few weeks, depending on who is available on account'a all the extra cleanup work after the storm."

"Not a problem. And thanks for your help." Lauren meant it. Sheila had been polite and helpful, like a receptionist ought to be. She figured Sheila's attitude adjustment no doubt stemmed from relief that she wouldn't have competition for Kyle's attention. Lauren had noticed how the girl eyed him when they'd all been in the office earlier, her calf's eyes betraying foolish thoughts. Kyle would never fall for this ninny.

On the way back to Mara's, Lauren decided to stop by Kyle's cottage, which was only slightly out of the way. She thought perhaps she'd left a few personal items behind when she'd scooted out so fast. She couldn't imagine what they might be, but after spending several nights at Kyle's in her muddled state of mind it was conceivable that she'd left an article or two of clothing.

At the cottage, she was thankful Kyle didn't lock his door. She knocked and called out in case he was home early. When no one answered, she entered and hurried through to the bedroom. She figured she was wasting precious time until she found a full set of her clothing, including underwear, freshly laundered and hanging inside the closet. Humiliated at the thought that he'd handled her soiled clothing, she felt nevertheless grateful that Kyle had made the effort to look after her so well. She took the clothing off the hangers and rolled them into a ball as an attempt to disguise the personal nature of the bundle rather than parade it along the mall.

She heard the front door open and called from the bedroom, "I'm in here,

Kyle, so don't be surprised. Don't shoot me. I'm not a burglar." *Not exactly, anyway.*

Kyle entered the room, frowning. "I heard you've made up your mind to leave and take your mother with you. Big mistake." He sat on the bed and patted a spot beside him for Lauren to sit.

She sat. "It wasn't an easy decision. You know that."

Kyle placed his arm across her shoulders. "I do know. I'm feeling sorry for myself, because I won't have the opportunity to see you again after tomorrow."

Lauren was surprised. She looked up into his eyes and smiled. "I didn't know you cared."

He encircled her with both arms before gently kissing the tip of her nose, then her lips. When she didn't resist, he pushed her gently backward onto the bed, then pulled up her legs so that she lay flat. He dropped to lie beside her before turning and taking her in his arms. "I've wanted to do this since I first met you." He planted a long, hard kiss on her lips.

Lauren had felt a shiver course through her body with the first kiss. She returned his kiss, then pulled away, laughing. "Would have been difficult with me—out of commission."

"True, but there were moments in-between. I never did believe you suffered from a communicable disease. I frankly thought it was from nerves. You've been under a lot of stress."

"Really? You're right about the stress, but I'm not the nervous type. I never once considered that possibility."

They both relaxed and lay there, side by side. After a few minutes, Kyle spoke. "It's not too late to change your mind."

His hand wandered along the curve of her breast, creating another shiver in Lauren. She turned to him. "I find you *very* attractive, Kyle. I wish we didn't live in such different worlds, but I don't see you moving to New York, nor could I move here."

"Why not?" he asked. "A lot of people work via the internet. Why couldn't you?"

"I considered it when I was here the first time. It wouldn't work. I need to be where the manuscripts arrive and to meet with agents and authors. I do a lot more than edit, you know. I wish you could see my office. No, I wouldn't want to work away from New York."

His hand had traveled to her thighs. She knew she had to make a move before this went further. "Oh, Kyle. I really could love you. I think you're a fine man, but it's the wrong time and the wrong place for us." She pulled away from his arms and got up from the bed.

He lay there looking defeated. She nearly melted at the sight of his boyish pout but forced herself to back away.

"I suppose you're right. But reconsider about your mother," he argued. "At least, we could see each other from time to time."

"Right, and in the meantime you would have fallen in love with someone else. Sheila, for one, has the hots for you."

Kyle laughed. "I took her to dinner once, but I haven't been able to work up the hots for her." He looked at Lauren's balled-up clothing. "What's that?"

She explained her attempt at modesty, eliciting his mocking laugh. "After all my hard work to wash and press your clothing. This is what you think of my effort?" He jumped up from the bed, grabbed her and planted another kiss on her lips.

Lauren didn't return the kiss this time but moved out of reach. "Sad as it is to say this, I need to get going."

"Oh, I forgot amidst my misplaced passion to tell you the results of the lab test on the papaya juice."

"What did you find out?"

"It's an odd thing, but the juice contained traces of ipecac. Did you add that for some reason?"

Lauren gasped. "Ipecac? No, but I'm sure I know who did."

— TWENTY-THREE —

LAUREN LEFT KYLE'S COTTAGE, intent on confronting Garrick to demand his purpose in adding ipecac to the papaya juice he'd supplied. After Kyle told her that Garrick was the one who sent the juice to her, she couldn't understand why Garrick had pretended that Kyle was the thoughtful provider.

She could see the truth now, in view of the large supply of juice Garrick kept on hand—and the damning evidence of the bottle of ipecac on the kitchen shelf. What on earth had he been thinking? Kyle had confirmed what she'd read on the label. The syrup is used to induce vomiting in cases of suspected poisoning, though now she realized that would not have been Garrick's purpose. What evil intent motivated the man to take such elaborate and downright mean steps? Was he acting out his Phelan persona? What did Garrick have to gain? Was it so important to convince her that Kyle was the snake Garrick believed him to be? Could lack of support from the officials after he and Mara pointed fingers at Kyle have driven him to make her ill in an attempt to scare her away from the man? Whatever his intent, it backfired because the sickness had driven her to Kyle for help.

Oh, God, she breathed. *What next?*

Garrick was no longer napping on the patio lounge. The screen door was unlocked and the door open, so she barged in to find the living room empty. She checked the bedroom. No sign of her mother. Mara was up and about somewhere.

Geoff called from the kitchen, "Who's there?"

"Where are they?" Lauren called, as she stepped into the kitchen. She found Geoff munching from the plethora of sandwiches. "Geoff, where's your father? I need to see him. And where's Mother?"

"Dad accompanied your mum over to her apartment." His haggard expression belied his attempt to act casual.

Lauren hated the idea of involving Geoff in this tangled mess but felt she had no choice, seeing as his father was the perpetrator of a foul deed. "Why, why on earth would your father put ipecac in the juice he was sending for me to drink, then telling me Kyle sent it? It made me terribly ill, and I can't help but believe he had a malicious intent." There, it was out. All of it.

Geoff set his sandwich aside and took her by the arm. "Sit down and tell me calmly what in hell you are talking about."

Lauren let him guide her to a chair at the dinette table before unloading her newfound knowledge. She found it impossible to keep her anger under control.

"Whew!" Geoff said. "The old boy really has gone daft."

"He seemed to me like the only sane one around here until you came," Lauren said. "If he's crazy enough to pull a stunt like this, then I'm getting a whole new picture of what the pair of them observed on the mall that night."

"Let's confront him and get at the truth. It's hard to believe he could be vicious. He's frequently a grumpy old snark, but I've never known him, even at his worst, to intentionally harm a person."

"You said they've gone over to Mother's?"

"Yes, about half an hour ago. No telling what mischief they're into by now."

"Oh, God, mind-boggling. It's getting late, but maybe they haven't created too much mayhem—yet."

"One can hope. Let's go."

As they hurried toward Mara's apartment, Lauren said, "I haven't noticed Sundowner's symptoms in your father, but then I hadn't considered him a victim of dementia. Now, I'm not sure."

"No. I think the old boy is merely an evil genius, manipulating and controlling. That's bad enough without blaming it on dementia."

Through the wide-open apartment door, they could hear voices. "Sounds like they're arguing," Geoff said. "What's going on in here?" he called as they entered.

Garrick peered around the bedroom door. "We're having a slight dispute over a minor matter."

"Slight?" Geoff asked. "It sounded like World War III starting. What's the problem?"

"Mara says she isn't leaving. She refuses to pack any clothing."

"That's all right," Lauren intervened. "I've already packed for her." She pushed past Garrick to confront her mother.

Mara looked up from where she stood staring into a half-empty suitcase laid out on the bed. "There you are. It's about time. That man says I have to pack. I don't know what he's talking about. I'm not going anywhere."

Lauren groaned inwardly. "Yes, Mother. We are both leaving early tomorrow morning." She'd hoped not to be so open about their departure, realizing how stubborn Mara could be—and irrational. "And 'that man' is your friend Garrick, so please be nice to him." She wondered at her own words, since she'd come here to read him the riot act. Now, she was defending him. "You don't need to worry about packing. I've already taken care of that for you while you were napping."

Mara resumed taking lingerie from the suitcase and placing it in the dresser drawer.

Lauren attempted desperately to calm herself before tackling Garrick. She picked up a nightgown from the suitcase.

"What are you doing?" Mara shrieked, snatching the nightgown away from Lauren. "Who are you anyway?"

Lauren sighed. "Come, Mother. Let me make some hot tea, and we'll visit with our friends in the living room."

Mara looked suspicious. She growled, "What friends? I have no friends."

Geoff called to Lauren, "Want me to round up a tech?"

"I suppose. It's that time of day." She heard Geoff leave and tried to guide Mara to the living room.

Mara shrugged her off. "Don't touch me. I don't like to be touched."

"Mother, you can be so sweet. Why do you act this way?"

"Stop calling me Mother. I'm not your mother." Mara scurried to the bathroom and locked the door.

Garrick stood in the bedroom doorway with a smirk on his face. "Not so easy to push us old folks around, is it?" He turned to head for the front door.

Lauren followed him while taking a second to compose herself. "Garrick, come back here and sit down. We have a matter to discuss."

Garrick took a long swig from the coffee mug he carried as he turned from the front door to follow Lauren's pointed finger.

Whiskey, no doubt, Lauren thought. But he'll need it before I finish with him.

He sat on a straight-back chair next to the bedroom, looking to her like a petulant child. Before she could tackle him on his reasons for doctoring the papaya juice, Geoff and Kyle rushed into the apartment.

"I got lucky," Geoff said. "Kyle was passing by and I grabbed him."

"Yep," Kyle said. "I'm on my way to the apartments with meds for other residents, but I can take care of your mother." He picked a syringe and a vial out of a basket he carried. "Where is she?"

"In the bathroom," Lauren answered, wondering at his intent to use an injection rather than a pill. She started to ask.

"Emergency supplies. I read your look. This acts faster."

Garrick blocked Kyle from entering Mara's bedroom. "Don't you dare go near her, you bastard."

Kyle turned to Lauren, his eyebrows raised.

"Garrick, step aside," Lauren barked. "Mother needs medication, and Kyle is here to take care of her."

Garrick refused to budge. "He'll take care of her, all right. Get out of here!" He shook his fist at Kyle.

"Dad, please don't do this. Mara needs help, and this fellow is good enough to come to our aid."

"You have no idea what this man will do." Garrick waved away Kyle. "Now, get going."

Kyle looked apologetically at Lauren. "I'll call for one of the other techs." He picked up his basket to leave.

"I'm sorry, Kyle. But thank you for trying. Mother is still locked in the bathroom, so please tell the tech he'll have to deal with that problem, too."

Kyle laughed. "Don't worry. It's impossible to lock these bathroom doors, for that very reason. The locks can be sprung open from the outside."

"That's comforting to know," Lauren said, wondering how comforting she'd feel the next time she thought she'd locked the bathroom door.

Garrick removed himself to a lounge chair after Kyle left. "Now, what was the business you wanted to discuss, young lady?"

"I'll be back at your place, Dad," Geoff said. "I don't think I'm needed here, and I really do want to get you packed and ready to go early tomorrow."

Garrick waved him off. "If you say so."

Lauren could wait no longer. As soon as the door closed, she began. "Garrick." She took a deep breath. "I don't think you meant to do me any harm, but why did you lie to me about Kyle sending the papaya juice, and why …" She took another breath as her anger peaked. "Why on earth did you add ipecac to the juice, knowing it would cause me to become nauseated?"

"Dear girl, surely you don't think I would do such a thing."

"Garrick," her voice shook, "I *know* you did it, so don't pretend you didn't."

The old man let out a deep sigh and closed his eyes. "It was for your own good. I wanted you to stay away from that monster."

"Well, it did just the opposite. And Kyle took very good care of me. I don't for a minute believe he's a murderer." *But I do know you're crazy.* She reined in her plan of attack to stop and think. *How can I argue logically with this man who, if not demented, is not quite rational?*

"Your safety was not my only concern, you know," Garrick offered.

"Really? Did you think that causing me such misery as to appear poisoned would bring to light Kyle's alleged wrongdoing?"

Garrick snorted. "'Wrongdoing' is scarcely adequate to describe a brutal murder."

Lauren sighed. "Garrick, I want to believe you and Mother, but frankly it's a stretch. A huge stretch, and activities such as you've undertaken scarcely lend support to your credibility."

"So you say, but you were not here. We were."

"And you think my mother was in her right mind?"

"At that hour, who's to say? I can only tell you what we saw, and it was that man, Kyle, who was beating and strangling another man."

"Who 'we' have yet to identify. Right?"

Garrick heaved a deep sigh. "So far, yes."

"And you, at first, didn't believe your eyes. You thought your friend Phelan had returned."

Garrick looked uncomfortable. "I at times have visits from Phelan when I've been deeply asleep, drugged."

Or drunk, Lauren thought. Or both. "What made you think the man was Kyle?"

"Your mother identified him first, then I could readily see that she was correct."

"Searching your memory, right?"

"You needn't believe me, but what I saw was that idiot Kyle throttling a man."

A tap at the door interrupted their conversation. The tech had arrived to administer Mara's pills.

"May I come in?" he asked.

"Please. My mother is in the bathroom. You'll need to coax her out. She's angry with me."

"Not a problem," he said.

Lauren didn't remember seeing this young man previously. "I don't believe I know your name."

"Jason, I'm new here."

"Oh?" Garrick said, "and how did you get here? I understand transportation to this island has been halted."

"True, if you come by sea," Jason said, "but I flew with Kyle by helicopter. His trip was an emergency because he'd had to make a run to George Town for medicine. I hitched a ride."

"Lucky you," Garrick said. "Do you have my medications also? I can hardly wait."

"No, sir. Another tech has been assigned to you. One of the young women. Katie, I believe."

Garrick smiled. "Well. Things are looking up. I like Katie. Maybe I'll hang around after all."

Lauren frowned. "Scarcely the time for humor," she said, in a stage whisper Garrick could hear.

Jason tried the bathroom door. When it wouldn't budge, Lauren watched as he poked a small screwdriver into a hole that released a button on the handle assembly, and the door sprung open.

"Hello, Mrs. Edwards. Nap time."

"Go away," Mara shrieked. "Don't you understand when a person needs privacy?"

Lauren could see her sitting on the toilet stool lid, filing her fingernails.

"I'm most aware of that, ma'am," he said. My name is Jason. I'm new on the job, and I'm only here to help you."

"I don't care what your name is, and I don't need anyone's help. Get out of here."

"Bully," Lauren heard Garrick mutter from where he sat in the living room.

"I will be glad to do so, ma'am, if you'll only swallow this little pill and this cup of water." He'd filled a paper cup at the bathroom sink.

Mara set the emery board aside and reached for the cup. "Oh, all right, if it will get rid of you. And take those other people with you." She swallowed the pill and glared at him.

"Thank you, ma'am," Jason said as he backed out of the room. "I hope you'll feel better real soon."

"I'll feel better when you're out of my sight."

Jason saluted Garrick and Lauren as he left the apartment. "Call us if you need help."

"I'd best get over to my place," Garrick said. "See what my boy is up to."

"Packing, he said, which I've already done. But wait, I'm not finished with you."

"What more is there to tell? My intentions were good. I guess they misfired. Drove you into the loving arms of that asshole. I'm sorry. Please accept my apologies and assurances that, had I the matter to do over, I would do it again."

"I'm sure you would, Garrick. Go now, but consider some soul searching because you're on the wrong track. Very wrong."

✵ ✵ ✵

Fired up by anger, Lauren returned Mara's lingerie to the dresser drawers, while, Mara watched warily from her command post on the toilet. She appeared to have forgotten her ideas about unpacking her suitcase.

Lauren called to her, "Mother, it's getting late, and you haven't had your evening meal."

"I'm not hungry. And who are you to tell me when to eat?"

Lauren sighed, wondering if the pill was ever going to take effect. Maybe Jason had given her the wrong one. At any rate, Mara needed sustenance before going to bed for the long night ahead. Or short, depending on your point of view, she thought.

"I'll heat up a can of chicken and rice soup," Lauren said.

"Heat up anything you want. Just take it elsewhere."

This won't do, Lauren thought. She knew better than to attempt to strong-arm her mother, after the frustrating experience in New York, but coaxing would have no effect whatsoever. She decided to let the aroma of food convince Mara. If that didn't work, she'd put one of the power bars she'd seen in the kitchenette alongside Mara's bed hoping she would feel enough hunger that she would help herself to whatever sustenance the bar would provide. The only problem, Lauren realized, was that dementia patients lose their sense of hunger.

She really wanted to go back over to Garrick's for the night, so they could make a quick getaway in the morning. With Mara acting up, however, and as angry as she herself remained with Garrick, it was probably best to stay put. She'd call over to Geoff to explain and to go over the plans again for the morning.

She'd need to pack Mara's toiletries when her mother vacated the bathroom. She could slip those few items in the bag last. She zipped the empty suitcase closed and moved it out of sight. No point in risking that Mara would get in a stew at the sight of it. Luckily, she hadn't noticed those beside the front door.

Lauren opened a can of vegetable soup and heated it in the microwave. As Garrick had pointed out, she was surprised that a microwave was allowed. What havoc could her mother have created with a mismanaged microwave?

She found a box of crackers and a jar of peanut butter. “Dinner’s ready, Mom,” she called. “Well balanced or not, we won’t starve.”

The bedroom door slammed shut.

“Maybe later, then.” Lauren sighed and bit into a cracker.

Chapter

— TWENTY-FOUR —

MARA'S ALARM ENDED LAUREN's brutally long night at four a.m. She had slept little, waking often to fret about how their little group could accomplish the morning's trip. When she slept, she dreamed she was awake. Now, she lay for a few minutes with her eyes closed, unable to greet the day with enthusiasm. She had no doubt that Mara would continue to balk, and Garrick would find some way to screw up the escape. Though Mara had insisted that she didn't want to leave, Garrick couldn't leave fast enough. With his propensity to antagonize nearly everyone by his criticism on most any subject, today he would surely be in rare form.

Finally, she arose from where she'd slept on the sofa bed in the living room. She quickly stripped the linens and folded the bed back into a sofa before waking her mother. Lauren gently tapped Mara on the shoulder as she passed by on her way to the shower. "Time to wake up, Mom. We're going on a trip today."

"That's nice," Mara yawned. "I love to travel."

Lauren breathed with deep relief. *Off to a good start. Glad we're leaving early.*

While Mara took her time easing out of bed, Lauren quickly showered, then helped her mother into the shower. "I'll have your clothes laid out, so you won't have to worry about decisions."

"Thank you, dear. You're such a considerate daughter." Mara added, with the hint of a giggle, "I must have done something right somewhere along the line." She closed the shower door and began singing.

Lauren listened while she stripped Mara's bedding to make sure she hadn't hidden any valuable jewelry underneath, her "safe deposit box" she'd called it in New York. Sure enough, Lauren found a diamond bracelet and emerald earrings, which she slipped into her pocket to stow more securely later. She thought Mara had brought very little jewelry to the island, other than her wedding ring and a gold wristwatch. Finding this small stash was a surprise, but Lauren was glad she'd made the effort to search.

The song from the shower continued, becoming an improvised version of "Tomorrow" from the Broadway musical *Annie.*

Lauren stopped for time out to comb her still damp hair into respectability. She thought about using her blow dryer but didn't want to bother unpacking it. She smiled as she listened to her mother's song. *Pray, let us find that "Tomorrow" proves a better day. And this one too for starters.*

Mara called for assistance from the shower. "Where's my robe?"

"I—" Lauren caught herself from saying she'd packed it. "It's in the laundry. This big towel should do the job."

Mara grabbed the towel and frowned. "I like to wrap up in my robe while I have morning coffee."

The wall clock showed less than an hour before they needed to be at the dock. "We'll only have a quick cup of instant coffee this morning, Mom, and a bowl of cereal. We must hurry."

Mara rubbed the towel over her wet head before wrapping it around her small frame and stepping from the shower. "Where's my hair dryer?"

"You don't own a hair dryer. You always comb your hair into place, saying it's easier on your hair than drying it out with hot air. And I agree."

"This won't do. I can't have wet hair. I'll catch cold."

"That's not likely in this balmy climate." *Balmy being the operative word here. Bite your tongue, Lauren. You're not funny.* "Here, let me help you comb it into place. Your natural wave will take care of it. It worked for me. I'm lucky to have inherited your hair."

As Lauren coiffed Mara's curls, her mother smiled. "*I'm* the lucky one to have such a caring daughter, though I still wish I had my hair dryer."

When they at last sipped coffee from Styrofoam cups and ate cereal out of little cardboard containers, moistened with water as they had no milk, the phone rang. Lauren answered.

"Are you packed and ready to go?" Geoff asked.

"Just about. Mother has to finish dressing. Twenty minutes, tops."

"We'll meet you at the benches along the mall near the pathway leading down to the dock."

Lauren hung up and hurriedly assisted Mara into a light pantsuit, a cheerful lemon color embroidered with tiny bouquets of spring wildflowers.

"Do I look all right?" Mara asked.

"You look stunning." She zipped the last of Mara's toiletries into her bag. "We must hurry now."

"But I need more coffee."

"We'll have some while we're waiting for the boat. We have to get to the dock early to sign in and pay. Then we can worry about coffee."

"Are we going to George Town? I understand that city has fabulous shopping."

"Yes, we are going to George Town." *Enough information for now. At least, she's cooperating this morning. Don't upset her.*

Lauren left the keys on the kitchen counter and the two women departed for the dock.

✵ ✵ ✵

Garrick and Geoff stood beside the mall benches, Garrick shuffling impatiently. Lauren could read their body language from a distance.

"It's going to be a long day," she said to Mara.

As they approached, Garrick met them, taking Mara's hand. "It's about time," he said.

"C'mon, Dad, they're not late."

"Nearly. Come along." Garrick continued to hold Mara's hand to help her maneuver the rough and uneven stone steps leading down to the dock. Some steps wobbled, making the footing precarious. Lauren and Geoff struggled with the luggage.

"This is risky," Lauren said, "though an improvement over the path we took to reach The Grotto, and it least this one has a handrail." With both hands carrying bags, she used the handrail to lean against for support, to keep from falling whenever a step teetered and threw her off balance. "What a trip," she muttered.

"You'd think in this civilized society, the place could afford better steps," Geoff said, "or better yet an elevator."

"Surely, there's an elevator from the dock into the kitchen area," Lauren said. "I doubt that they carry hundred pound bags of rice and flour up these steps. And what about wheelchairs? Can you imagine taking a person in a wheelchair up and down these steep steps?"

"I'm sure you're right," Geoff agreed. "The problem is that we don't want to have to deal with Dickerson or any of his staff by asking permission. They would no doubt find ways to delay us on our mission out of here."

"Speaking of staff," Garrick called over his shoulder to Lauren, "where's your boyfriend today? Sleeping in after more nighttime activity?"

Lauren gritted her teeth and ignored the question.

Geoff, following her, leaned forward and whispered, "Please don't kick him down the steps."

"I'm tempted, but I don't want to injure my mother."

At last, reaching the dock, the foursome looked around. The shuttle boat hadn't arrived, but the window at the dock office was open.

Geoff approached the harbormaster. "We have reservations."

"Let's see your passports," the man replied.

Lauren pulled her passport from the large shoulder bag she carried and handed it over. She reached into the envelope Sheila had given her with Mara's release papers. "Oh, no!" Lauren cried. "This isn't Mother's passport. It's for someone named Elise O'Brien." She emptied the envelope onto the counter, but other than the release papers no other passport fell out. "I stupidly forgot to check to make sure it was the right one."

Taking a quick look at Garrick's passport, Geoff confirmed, "It's his all right. I hadn't thought to check either."

"Oh, Geoff, what do we do now?"

"What's the delay?" Garrick called from where he and Mara sat at the edge of the pier.

"Just a minute, Dad." Geoff turned to Lauren. "Not much choice. You'd better get up to the office and pound it out of them." He looked at his watch. "The night staff is still on duty. Maybe they'll cooperate, for a change. I'd do it for you, but they'll probably require your presence to sign for it."

"They already have my signature."

"True, but we don't need any bureaucratic complications at this point."

Lauren agreed. "I wish you could come with me, but you'd better stay and keep an eye on those two."

"Righto. Here's my cell phone number. Call if you run into trouble."

"I feel like an idiot."

Geoff grinned, though revealing sympathy in his eyes. "I'd like to disagree, but ..."

Lauren hurried up the craggy steps, stumbling several times despite clutching the handrail. At the top, she paused to catch her breath. Checking her wristwatch, she saw it was a little after six o'clock. She wasn't sure what hour the staff changeover took place but thought Geoff was probably right about it being at seven—and judging from the hour Kyle had left for work each morning.

Rushing toward the administration office, she suddenly felt a hand squeeze her shoulder. Startled, she whirled around, "Geoff, you shouldn't—" Instead, she found Kyle standing before her. "Oh! You're up early."

"I might say the same to you."

"You knew we're to leave today."

"Mmm. When I saw you, I thought you'd changed your mind. Maybe 'hoped' is a better word."

His sad, hazel eyes sought hers, and Lauren felt a momentary tenderness for this dear man, who had been so badly maligned. "I have to hurry. I need Mother's passport."

"I thought you'd taken care of that."

"So did I." She explained the mix-up, while hurrying toward the office, Kyle keeping pace with her.

"Uh-oh. Maybe I can help you speed things up."

"Please. They'll listen to you."

"Let's hope. Where's the rest of the gang?"

"Down on the dock. I really screwed up."

"It happens. We'll get it straightened out."

They found the door to the office locked. "I guess the night guys knocked off early," Kyle said. "I don't have a key to these offices, so we'll have to wait."

"When do you go on duty?"

"Not for another hour. I'll stick with you."

"That's kind of you, but I'm running the risk of missing the shuttle."

"True."

"Can you get hold of Dickerson for me? Or one of the day staff who would be willing to come in early?"

"Calling Dickerson would be a bad idea. He has a nasty temper, in case you haven't noticed, and he doesn't usually show up before ten o'clock. I understand he stays up most of the night and sleeps in late. I doubt that Sheila would cooperate without his say-so."

"It's her oversight in the first place that created my problem. She ought to be willing to help."

"You think she'd see it that way?"

Lauren took the cell phone from her purse and punched in Geoff's number. When he answered, she explained the situation. "If I can't get back fast enough," she said, "you'd better go ahead without us."

Kyle spoke up. "I'll go down and help your mother climb up the steps, if it's necessary."

Lauren nodded.

"I heard him," Geoff said. "I gather whatshisname showed up."

"Yes, Kyle is here, but he's powerless to get in the office to pick up the passport. It looks like we're stuck." She could hear the shuttle boat's horn sounding in the distance. Verging on tears, she said, "Geoff, it's all right. Go. You need to get Garrick out of here, and we'll be all right for another day. Kyle said he'll come down for Mother."

"I don't feel good about this Lauren, and the old boy will blow his top. He's already giving me a fishy look—while holding tight to your mother's hand."

Lauren heard a louder blast from the catamaran as it approached the island. A tear stole down her cheek. "You have my address, Geoff. Please keep in touch. I wish you and Garrick the very best."

"If you insist. I'll cross my fingers that you get this resolved before we pull out of here. I'll see what I can do to delay departure, but don't count on my ability to interfere with their schedule."

Chapter
— TWENTY-FIVE —

LAUREN HESITATED OVER ACCEPTING Kyle's offer to help bring Mara up the steep stairs from the dock. Mara might freak out altogether at the sight of the man. On the other hand, if Lauren left the office area and the employees showed up early, she would be wasting precious time when the two might still be able to catch the boat. What to do? One more dilemma, but this one was self-imposed. She couldn't leave Mara alone on the dock after the men departed. No telling what she might think up for entertainment while the harbormaster was busy. At the absolute least, she'd be frightened.

Lauren called Geoff's cell phone again and asked if he had time to walk Mara part way up the steps. She could meet her mother while Kyle watched the office for activity. She gave Kyle her cell phone number to call if it appeared there was a chance she could get the passport while they could still catch the shuttle.

"Here's Elise O'Brien's passport, in case you're allowed to make the swap before I return."

"Sure, then I'll run it down to you."

Geoff had walked Mara past the mid-point of the stairway by the time

Lauren reached them. "Thanks so much, Geoff. I've got her now. Take care of yourselves. I'd give you a hug if I could reach past Mom."

"Save it for New York," he said, smiling. "I made reservations for you both to leave on the morning shuttle and checked your bags. I didn't think you'd be wanting to take your mum over in the late afternoon."

"Good point. We can probably use her apartment for another night. If not, I'll rent guest quarters."

"I'll make hotel reservations for you when we reach George Town, if you wish. That way I could check to see if the hotel is reputable."

"You're too good, Geoff. But what about your flight? I don't want to hold you up. I can make our reservations while I wait here. Take my chances on space and quality."

"Fine, then. Neither Dad nor I feel good about deserting you, so text me, if you will. We want to be sure you get off this fu—". He looked at Mara. "Lovely little island." He grinned, waved and returned to the dock.

As the women began their climb, Lauren following, Mara called over her shoulder, "Why are we doing all this exercise? I'm not so young anymore, you know, and climbing up and down these awful steps is not my idea of healthy."

"I'm sorry, Mom. My mistake. We're not leaving until tomorrow."

Mara stopped and turned to look Lauren square in the face. "You mean we're missing a day of shopping in George Town? Are you crazy? Why would we stay behind while the men go ahead and have all the fun?" She stopped and giggled. "Oh, I get it. They've lined up some girls. I guess they find us boring. Too bad."

Lauren took a deep breath to calm her nerves. "It's not what you think. I screwed up, Mom. I didn't get your passport, so we can't board the boat."

"Oh, my. That's not like you, dear."

"I hope not."

As they walked toward the office, Kyle hurried toward them.

"Sheila just arrived. I told her the problem."

"And she laughed, I'll bet."

"Not quite. But she said you'd have to come in to make the swap yourself. She can only release the passport to you."

"How good of her. Do you mind if I punch her out?"

"Calm down, hon'. It won't help to rough her up."

Lauren turned toward Mara, walking beside her, in time to see a murderous look take aim toward Kyle. She squeezed Mara's arm to reassure her. "Kyle is helping us," she whispered, grateful that Mara had retained good hearing.

"I'll bet."

"Be nice."

Mara grunted.

In the office, Sheila had located Mara's passport and placed it on the counter. "Sorry about that," she said without looking up from her computer.

Lauren bit her tongue as she swapped the O'Brien woman's passport for Mara's. "You might be searching for this some day."

"Nah. She died a couple of years ago. Don't ask me how her passport got in the wrong file. Gremlins, I guess." She continued typing.

"Where was my mother's? In the O'Brien file?"

"It had slipped out of the file folder and was wedged down underneath other files in the drawer."

Lauren accepted the explanation without comment, chalking it up, as no big surprise, to sloppy clerical work.

She heard the horn blast from the shuttle, signaling its departure. That's that, she thought. We won't get away from here today.

"Sheila, we won't be leaving until tomorrow morning, so may we still have access to Mara's apartment until then?"

"Sorry. The crew's already in your mother's unit taking out the furniture for cleaning."

Alarmed by this news, Lauren asked, "What about the clothing and personal articles in drawers?"

"Don't worry, that stuff will be stored in cartons for later shipping."

Kyle intervened. "You can use my place. I'll be working, so you'll have it to yourselves."

"Problem solved," Sheila said.

"I don't think we should impose any further on this good man." Lauren was uncomfortable with the idea of staying in Kyle's cottage. How would Mara react when she discovered where they were? "Can we rent a guest suite for the night?"

"Sorry, those that aren't already booked are being renovated. Better take Kyle up on his offer."

Kyle laid his arm across Lauren's shoulders. "See? Everything works for the best."

She chose not to comment. Things surely hadn't worked out best for Mara and herself. "Kyle, we'll be over a little later then. And thanks. Come on, Mom. Let's get a little more breakfast."

"You'll have to pay cash, you know," Sheila said, back to her standard smugness. "She's no longer a resident, and visitors have to pay cash."

"I see. We'll manage."

Kyle ushered them from the office and handed Lauren his employee card. "Here, use this. I'll treat. In the meanwhile, I'm off on rounds. See you later." He chucked Lauren under the chin. "Can't say I'm sorry about the delay."

Chapter

TWENTY-SIX

COFFEE AND A COMFORTING cinnamon bun rounded out the morning's breakfast before Lauren led Mara along the mall to Kyle's cottage. She was pleased that Geoff had volunteered to check their bags with the harbormaster so they wouldn't have to haul the heavy things up and down those awful steps. She was relieved, too, that she wouldn't have to drag the luggage around the grounds. On the other hand, what would they do tonight for bedtime clothing and toiletries? She'd be damned if she'd ask Sheila again for access to Mara's cottage, even to try to rescue personal items not yet packed up and carted off to storage.

She was fond of Kyle, but she wouldn't want to share his toothbrush—or sleep naked—or in her street clothes. Come to think of it, he might still have the toothbrush he'd so thoughtfully provided earlier in the week, and perhaps he'd have another for Mara. Maybe he could hustle up a couple of hospital gowns plus some personal items from the company store. She'd seen the store housed in the administration building, but she understood it was only for use by employees or monitored residents. Heaven help visitors in need, but there must be exceptions. She'd ask Kyle. She still had enough cash, but she'd try to use her credit card. Fortunately, U. S. currency and credit cards were accepted in this British protectorate. She'd worry about the clothing problem later. She was glad at least that she'd kept a supply of Mara's medications in her purse.

At Kyle's cottage with its unlocked door, entry was no problem. Mara stopped, looked confused. "Why are we here? Can we walk right in like this?"

"Of course. Our friend loaned us his cottage."

Once Lauren convinced her to go inside, Mara looked around at the oil paintings hanging on the walls, studied the ceramic figures and glass bowls. "Very nice," she said. "Our friend has good taste. Who is this friend, anyway? Is Garrick joining us?"

"No, Mom, Garrick and his son had to leave without us. We'll stay here until tomorrow." She'd hold off identifying "our friend" as long as she could. Get Mara settled first.

"Whatever you say, dear. I trust your judgment."

"Mmm." *I wish I could trust my own.*

"My, but we've had an energetic morning," Mara said. "I'm ready for a nap."

"That's good. It will be a long day, so napping will make it go faster."

"I guess I don't understand what all this fuss is about."

"I'll explain later, Mom." *Again.* "You can stretch out here in the bedroom." She led the way to Kyle's bed. "You'll find it most comfortable."

"Why can't I nap in my own bed?" She stopped and looked at Lauren with suspicion. "And how do you know it's so comfortable?"

"Long story. We'll save it for later." *Maybe.* "Here's a light blanket."

Lauren had hoped Mara wouldn't slip into her anxieties so early. It wasn't quite ten o'clock but with all the commotion and exercise the mood and personality changes seemed to be arriving early. This could be a very long day.

Mara kicked off her shoes and stretched out on the bed. "This is a beautiful bedspread with all the big, colorful flowers. Our friend must be well-to-do. Burian likes tropical flowers. They would keep him awake but not me." She yawned. "I hope our friend doesn't mind my lying on top of this nice bedspread."

"He won't mind. He'll be pleased, if I know him. He's a most generous person." Lauren tucked the blanket around Mara's shoulders and stretched it over her feet. She kissed her mother's forehead, watched her sink quickly into sound sleep.

Lauren studied her mother's sweet face and thought how sad it was that she'd fallen so far into dementia. Mara still retained fragments of the bright, happy person she had once been despite slipping daily into less and less comprehension of the real world around her and, sadly, at times not even recognizing her own daughter. *If only she would lose that old Burian. We could all do without him rearing up. Talk about ugly. She can't remember me, but she has Burian front and center stage often enough.*

Where will it end? Lauren asked herself. She knew taking her mother to New York was a bad idea. Even in a group home with decent care, Mara's world was closing down. Regardless, she could no longer remain in this cesspool, where even the management seemed confused. At least, Mara had been happy here for a while. Lauren wondered if she would miss her friendship with Garrick, or would she even remember him? Fussy old budget that he was, he had some redeeming qualities.

Lauren stepped back into the living room. She knew her attempts to brainwash Mara with good thoughts about Kyle would be useless, but she felt better for making the effort. Strange how Mara had latched onto the idea that Kyle was a vicious murderer, though strong reinforcement by Garrick could explain that. With the fantasies both entertained nightly, it seemed, who in their right mind could believe them?

She settled down on the sofa to try to ease her troubled mind with a nap of her own. She had no sooner closed her eyes and relaxed than the door opened, and Kyle rushed into the room.

"Hey," he said. "Guess what! Dickerson came into the office early, and I talked him into giving me the day off so I could entertain you two. Surprisingly, he went for the idea without an argument." He stopped and chuckled, "I think he wants me to keep you two out of his hair."

Lauren gave him a weak smile. "What do you propose to do to entertain us? Mother is sleeping, and I was just about to nod off."

He knelt beside her and cupped her face tenderly in his hand. "I can think of a number of ways." The hand moved to her breast and she sat up.

"I'll bet you can," she laughed. "But my chaperone is nearby."

"Sleeping, you said."

He kissed her lips, and she felt a return of the earlier stirring that made her want to surrender all self-control. "Oh, Kyle. Like I told you, it's the wrong time."

"It seems right to me." He pushed her gently back and kissed her again. "What would you think if I left here and moved to New York?"

She sat up again, forcefully. "You'd do that for me?"

"In a second."

"How would you earn a living?"

"I'm a man of many talents, as I keep trying to tell you. I would find work in the medical field. And it would no doubt pay better than here. The scenery might not be as romantic, but … one compromises when one must."

Lauren laughed. "You're beginning to sound like Garrick." She took his face in both hands and kissed him soundly on the lips. "How soon could you go?"

"Would tomorrow be too soon?"

"You could leave with us in the morning?" Lauren's enthusiasm was growing. "But you don't have airline tickets."

"Let me worry about that."

"Geoff said he had rebooked my flight and added Mother's, but I'll follow up in case we need to make adjustments after you verify arrangements for your trip. When will you talk to Dickerson?"

"I may not have an opportunity. He said he was flying over to George Town as soon as he could get away. I haven't heard the helicopter, but then I haven't been paying attention. What I'll do is just walk off the job. I picked up my weekly pay this morning, so … services rendered."

"That won't look good on your resumé."

"Let me worry about that."

Mara appeared in the bedroom doorway. "What's all this racket?" She frowned at Kyle, who held Lauren in his arms. "Who are you? And what are you doing to this woman?"

"Uh-oh," Lauren said.

"Yep, looks like time for meds."

"It's early. I hate to keep drugging her like this."

"I know, but it's best. With a light dose, she'll calm down, and it will be easier on all of us."

Lauren found her purse and brought out the vial of pills she'd picked up in the office. Kyle cut a pill in half and handed it to Lauren with a glass of water. "Here, Mom," she said, "this will make you feel better."

"I feel just fine right now. You take them."

"I've already taken mine."

"And do you feel better?"

"Immensely."

Mara took the pill from Lauren's hand and swallowed it with one big gulp of water. "I still don't know who you two are or what you're doing in my apartment."

Kyle intervened. "Tell you what. Let's go on a picnic. It's a nice day, and it will get us all out of this stuffy place."

Mara brightened. "I love picnics."

"I don't know," Lauren said. "The last one didn't turn out well."

"True," Kyle agreed. "This time it will be perfect. We can plan our new tomorrow beside the dazzling blue sea."

"No, you're not thinking of going to The Grotto again?" Lauren asked.

"Sure am. Our fun was interrupted last time, but I want you to remember how beautiful that particular spot can be, to erase the bad memories. Last chance?"

"Well … I suppose so. It would get us out of a long and tedious afternoon. At least it will be private, providing we don't dredge up any more corpses."

"I guarantee you we won't see a one. I was down there yesterday, and the place was quiet as a tomb."

"You sure have a way with words. That's not quite a convincing argument."

Kyle chuckled. "I'll round up enough food, and later we'll climb back up here to enjoy the long evening and romantic sunset."

Lauren shook her head in amazement at her willingness to go along with this wacky idea. On the other hand, what else was there to do on a very long day? Watch TV? No thanks. "Mom, are you okay with this?"

Mara, who sat primly upright on a straight chair, merely stared at her. "Who is this 'Mom' you keep speaking to? I don't see any other women around here. Just that ugly man."

"Mom, be polite. Kyle is a beautiful man." She smiled at Kyle, who winked at her. "He's kind and helpful, and he's our friend. He's going with us to New York."

"What are you talking about? I'm not going anywhere with you people."

"Go, Kyle. Fetch. Maybe a picnic is just what we need."

"Woof." Kyle panted like a dog as he trotted toward the door, calling over his shoulder, "I didn't think I was *that* ugly."

Chapter

— TWENTY-SEVEN —

MARA DOZED, NEARLY SLIPPING from the chair where she waited while Kyle rounded up food for the picnic. She'd refused to return to the bedroom, saying she needed to keep an eye on whatever was going on in the place. Lauren, sitting opposite, caught and held her in place.

Awakening at the touch, Mara's confusion surfaced. She stared suspiciously at Lauren and shook herself free. "Go away."

"Mom, wouldn't you rather lie down?"

"What? Do you think I can't take care of myself? Leave me alone." She stood slowly and stiffly before wandering into the bedroom to throw herself across the king-size bed. She was sleeping before Lauren could say more, so she tucked the blanket over her mother once again.

Unable to relax, Lauren thought through the plans for the day. The Grotto. Wasn't that the last place on earth she ever hoped to revisit? Why did she let Kyle talk her into going back there? Surely, there were more scenic spots along the beach that would be private enough. And what about his plan to ditch his job and go with her to New York? She'd been carried away with his smooth talk—and his manly persuasion—but was this the direction she wanted for her life? She would be tied to him, or vice-versa. Of course, he could be useful when it came to knowledgeable care for Mara. But at what cost? Things were moving too fast—or not at all, when it came to getting away from this island.

She felt exhausted after the night of little sleep, and now all she wanted was to close her eyes and space out. If it weren't so early in the day, she'd look for a bottle of wine and have a little nip. Kyle surely kept wine on hand. It might help her relax. As she pondered pursuing this course, Lauren drifted into sleep.

❋ ❋ ❋

Kyle awoke her with a gentle shake of her shoulder. "Wake up, Sleeping Beauty. Prince Charming has returned."

"What? Oh, Kyle. I guess I fell asleep."

"Brilliant deduction. It's after one o'clock, and I left here at ten."

"What have you been doing? Oh, you went off to pick up food for a picnic."

"That, and I found that Samuel was drafted into duty taking over my rounds, so I pitched in to help him. I knew your mom needed rest, but I didn't mean to stay away so long. I'm sorry, if you worried."

Lauren laughed. "I thought you'd changed your mind, that you were going to desert us after all." *Liar, you slept the whole time he was away.*

"Not for a minute would I desert you."

"Really?" Lauren looked at her wristwatch.

"Well, for a couple of hours, but you were always in my heart, darlin'." He held his hand over his heart and kissed her on the cheek.

"Men!"

Mara staggered into the living room rubbing sleep from her eyes. "Where am I?"

Lauren explained their plans while evading a reply to her question.

Mara's eyes brightened as before at the mention of the picnic. Then she looked around the room suspiciously. "Who's going?"

"Just we three, Mom."

Mara shook her head. "I guess that's all right. I don't usually go on picnics with strangers."

Lauren drew a deep breath. "We're friends, and we promise to be nice. You'll have a good time with us."

"I hope so." Mara headed to the bathroom. "I'd like to take a shower first. I just woke up."

"But you had one this morning. Oh, well, go ahead if it makes you feel better."

Mara closed and locked the bathroom door.

"I hope we can avoid picking the lock this time," Lauren said.

"Don't worry. My bathroom door lock can be sprung, too."

✵ ✵ ✵

As the three set off across the mall, Kyle hurried them along. Lauren had vetoed the idea of taking the long way around "to say fond farewells to favorite sites," as Kyle expressed it. She knew from their earlier experience that the path down to The Grotto would be tiring enough for Mara so didn't care to push the idea of unnecessary exercise. After all, they'd both already been up and down the path to the boat dock today. She didn't feel stress in her legs, but then she was much younger than the mother who had given birth to her at mid-life. Plus, she doubted that Mara would remember any "favorite sites" once they departed the island.

Kyle carried the picnic basket, which he'd packed lighter this time. He kept a firm grip on Mara's hand as they picked their way down the rocky path. Lauren carried both small blankets this time. She was surprised her mother didn't object to Kyle's assistance, but Mara seemed grateful, a good sign. Perhaps this picnic wouldn't end in disaster.

The jungle-like shrubbery near the pathway had seemed attractive, if precarious, on their previous descent. This time, Lauren viewed the lush growth as ominous, wondering what she was thinking when she'd agreed to revisit what had turned into a grim experience on their first outing.

Mara slipped several times but by grasping Kyle's hand and arm avoided a fall. She seemed to enjoy the challenge. Lauren, behind the two, managed to keep her footing but realized her legs were stronger and her shoes better suited for hiking than Mara's sandals. No one had expected Mara to need hiking shoes when she'd moved to the island.

When they reached the beach, Kyle spread the blankets over the sand in the shade of a palm tree. "Here you go," he said to Mara. "I wish I had a chair for you, but this is the best I can do."

"It's just fine," Mara said, settling herself daintily at the edge of the blanket. "I'm spryer than you might think I'd be for an old girl—and I'm hungry."

Lauren looked on in amazement. She'd expected Mara to be hostile and frightened by these "strangers" who'd dragged her down the side of the cliff, expected her to complain about the physical stress. No accounting for the power of a picnic in her mother's mind. She'd been a promoter of such events her entire life, and if one gave her peace now, so be it. Or maybe exercise was what she'd needed all along.

Kyle settled beside Mara and patted a spot for Lauren to join them.

"I don't often party with strangers," Mara said. She looked at Kyle. "But you seem very nice. Is that woman your wife?"

He grinned and winked at Lauren. "Not yet."

Lauren winced and sat beside Mara, thinking that the exercise hadn't done as much good as she'd hoped. At least, Mara was in an upbeat frame of mind, something for which she could be grateful.

"We're like a happy little family." Mara's tinkling laughter brought a note of gaiety to the party.

Kyle laughed. "I'll drink to that!" He raised a bottle of beer he'd opened and clinked it against Lauren's can of Coke. "And here's our surprise for lunch. Roast beef sandwiches!"

"Good," Mara said. "Not one of those old fishy things."

After they ate quietly and eagerly, Kyle picked up the remains and set it aside so the three could stretch out side-by-side on the palm-shaded blankets, their bodies touching. Lauren was surprised that Mara didn't object to the closeness, but her mother looked serene and had fallen into a contented doze. Lauren and Kyle lay quietly, holding hands.

Before long, a cloud passed over the sun, darkening the blue sea that seemed to stretch so endlessly before them. A sudden rush of wind whipped the fronds of the palm trees.

Lauren sat up and looked around. "Maybe we should start back. It seems we're in for an afternoon squall."

"Nah, it'll blow over," Kyle said.

Mara opened her eyes but lay still, a smile on her face and seemingly oblivious to Lauren's concern or Kyle's reassurances.

Minutes later, the first splats of rain dampened the party. A flash of lightning and crash of thunder followed.

"Guess I was wrong about the blowing over part." Kyle grabbed Mara's arm and pulled her to her feet.

Lauren assisted Mara while Kyle bundled their trash and the utensils into the blankets.

"C'mon," he said, grabbing Lauren around the waist while she hung on to Mara. "We'll run for The Grotto."

"Oh, geez," Lauren said. "I'd just about rather wait it out in the rain." Nevertheless, the three stumbled to the mouth of the cavern.

"I hope you have a flashlight," Lauren said.

"In my pocket," he answered. "Hurry, get inside. The lightning is getting closer."

Once in the shelter of The Grotto, Kyle fished for the flashlight. "Let's get further inside," he said. He shined the light on Mara. "I hope you didn't get too wet."

"Just a little," she said, shivering. "I'm getting cold."

"Here." Kyle dumped the picnic trappings and wrapped a blanket around Mara. "It's a little damp but not soaked. It should help."

"Yes, I feel better already. Who are you young man?"

Lauren sighed. "He's our friend, Mom. He's taking good care of us."

Mara moved away from them and looked around. "It's dark in here." She kept walking deeper into the cave.

A flickering light appeared in the distance. "I see you now, Burian. But you can't scare me."

"I don't intend to scare you," the deep, male voice answered from the depths of the blackness. "Follow me."

Mara complied, dropping the blanket from her shoulders while walking toward the light and the familiar voice.

— TWENTY-EIGHT —

"MOTHER! STOP!" LAUREN CRIED, racing toward Mara, who was disappearing into the darkness.

"Wait," Kyle said, grabbing Lauren around the waist to restrain her.

Lauren tore at his hands. "Who is that man? I swear I've heard his voice."

"It's not Burian."

"Please, let me go. Whoever he is, he might harm her."

"We'll go together." He grabbed the flashlight while clutching Lauren tightly to his side.

"You didn't tell us someone would be down here."

"I didn't know anyone would be here."

They hurried together deeper into The Grotto. The flashlight cast a weak beam over the rough ground.

"Have you ever been deep inside this cavern?" Lauren's voice trembled.

"No, I've only explored the outer area where we came in …"

"And where we found the dead man," Lauren finished.

Kyle reached in his pocket for his cell phone. "No signal. Shit! Do you have yours?"

"It's in my purse. I dropped it at the entrance to the cave."

"We may have to go back and try to get a signal outside."

"No, no. We can't wait. We have to get my mother out of here. Please!"

"I wish I had a gun. I don't like this."

"Hurry, Kyle, they're still ahead. I can't see his light—or my mother!" Lauren tried to control the building hysteria.

She stumbled in a pool of water and screamed. "Oh! Blood!"

"No, it's only water dripping from above," Kyle answered, shining his flashlight across the ground as he helped her to her feet. "Hurry."

Lauren had never in her life felt so frightened and helpless. She could still hear shuffling footsteps ahead and the tinkle of her mother's laughter.

"At least, he hasn't harmed her," Kyle said.

"Yet," Lauren added.

They moved as quickly as possible over the hard, lumpy ground, interspersed with more patches of mud caused by water leaking from above. Always, the sound of voices preceded them. The sudden fluttering of wings and rush of air overhead caused Lauren to lean in to Kyle for safety.

"Bats, of course," he said. "I'm surprised we haven't flushed out more and sooner."

"Ohhh," Lauren cried, swatting at her hair.

"They won't hurt you if we leave them alone. They're more afraid of us."

"What level of hell is this?" she asked.

"Shhh. We don't want him to hear us."

They came up against a solid wall. Shining the flashlight around, Kyle found a low opening that he proceeded to crawl through. Lauren started to follow.

"No," he said. "Let me find out where this leads. If I don't come back, run for help."

He disappeared, taking the flashlight with him. Lauren sat in the dark, wondering how she would ever find her way out. More fluttering of wings. She made a decision.

She felt around the wall to locate the hole where Kyle had crawled through, then eased herself into it. She heard no sounds but a faint glow in the distance gave off enough light for her to see ground that was fairly level. She wouldn't be stepping off a cliff into an abyss.

Lauren moved toward the light. She rounded a corner and saw before her a table-like rock, altar-like and lit by the flame from a sconce mounted on the wall. On the flat surface of the rock, her mother lay motionless, appearing unconscious. A man in a hood and cape stood over her, babbling loudly with words that made no sense to Lauren. Both of the man's hands joined together to hold a large hunter's knife raised above Mara's breast, poised to strike.

"Oh," she cried, "Don't—" She hit the ground, knocked off her feet by Kyle, who covered her mouth with his hand. The man didn't appear to have heard her, his voice loud, but his words still unintelligible. Kyle pulled her back around the corner.

"Be quiet," he whispered.

"He's going to kill her!"

"I hope he's only playing some kind of sick game to scare her—and give himself a thrill."

"She's already unconscious."

"Or acting out a Burian fantasy. Do you see who he is?"

Lauren peeked around the corner again. The hood had slipped from the man's head. "Dickerson!" she cried. Kyle clapped his hand over her mouth again.

"Listen to me," Kyle said. "After I crawl around the edge to the right, doing my best to keep out of sight, you distract him by standing where he can see you and scream your head off. First, give me a couple of minutes and don't get too close. I'm going to try to rush him, get the knife away. Knock him out if I have to. If I find a drug he used, I'll force it on him, and we'll get them both out of here.

Lauren let out a deep breath. "We have no choice."

Kyle left her side and disappeared behind a low rock formation. She waited as long as she could bear. Seconds seemed like minutes. When she could wait no longer, she crept around the corner and moved close enough, she hoped, to be seen but far away enough to be out of the knife's range, unless Dickerson was a very experienced marksman.

Lauren stood up and began screaming bloody murder. She spotted Kyle as he slithered around the side of the altar-rock.

At her scream, Dickerson stopped chanting and looked up toward her, the knife still in his hand. Kyle, now hunched over, raced behind the altar and disappeared. Dickerson dropped out of sight with a blood-curdling shriek.

Lauren stared, struck dumb. Then she rushed to her mother's side. Mara lay still on the flat rock, but she was breathing.

Kyle stood up behind the altar, leaned against it, panting, with blood on his hands and dripping from his face. His face contorted in anguish as he struggled to find words. "He fell on it. He fell on the knife."

Lauren hurried around the rock to where Kyle now knelt beside Dickerson's lifeless body.

Kyle looked up. "The knife must have sliced through a major artery." Blood spurted from Dickerson's neck, the knife still lodged firmly near his throat. Kyle removed the knife and applied pressure to close the wound and stop the flow of blood.

Lauren watched the effort for long, long minutes, an eon, it seemed. She held Mara's hand, though she too appeared lifeless.

After again checking Dickerson's pulse, Kyle stood up, wiping the gore from his hands onto his white shorts and pulling the shirt up over his face to wipe away blood and sweat. He held it there for long seconds before lowering it and finding words. "He's gone."

"The man was completely mad," Lauren breathed.

"No doubt about it."

They turned to look at Mara, who was beginning to stir. Kyle felt her pulse then lifted her into his arms. "She'll be all right. Let's get out of here. There's something I need to tell you. Bring the flashlight and follow me."

Chapter

— TWENTY-NINE —

AFTER STRUGGLING TO REACH the small opening to the outer cave, Kyle and Lauren cautiously eased Mara through the hole. Kyle lifted her in his arms and deposited her gently on the slightly damp blankets near the entry to The Grotto. He pulled a picnic cloth from the food basket and slipped it under her head and shoulders. "Her clothing is dry, so she should be all right until we get help down here," he called to Lauren. "The rain has stopped, but the beach is still wet and the path, no doubt, slippery."

Lauren caught up with Kyle to kneel beside her mother as he stepped outside to try his cell phone again. This time, the phone activated, and she heard him place a call.

Returning inside, he said, "I called for help and asked for a couple of stretchers in case you don't think you can manage to climb the path." He pushed her hair back from her brow. "You've been through a lot."

"I'm okay. I can walk. You said you have something to tell me. What is it, Kyle?" Her suspicions were rampant. What was Kyle mixed up in? She checked her mother again before standing up to face the man. Mara was now breathing normally and beginning to show signs of regaining consciousness.

"Your mother and Garrick were not wrong when they reported seeing me on the mall that night, beating a man."

"What?" She backed away from him. "Are you telling me you killed a patient?"

"No, I'm not telling you that. The man was Sheila's husband, Shannon. He was an inmate here, a paranoid schizophrenic and extremely violent at times. He escaped while I was trying to help him bathe, so I chased and grabbed him. He struggled, we fought, and I had to knock him out."

"In the middle of the night?"

"Yes. Sometimes cold showers were the only way we could keep him under control. Obviously, this time it didn't work."

"Is he dead? Did you strangle him?"

"He is dead. I did not strangle him, though it may have appeared so from a distance. I had my hands on his shoulders before slugging him."

"But you didn't kill him?"

"No, I did not. I left him on the ground, unconscious, while I ran to report to Dickerson what had happened. He'd heard the commotion and was already outside. He ordered me to get Shannon back into the building. I returned and dragged him from the mall to the infirmary where I left him for medication and further treatment."

Lauren covered her face with her hands. "I'm relieved to hear that."

"But that's not all."

Lauren looked up. "Please tell me the rest."

"The body we found down here that first time, that was Shannon."

"You recognized him and didn't tell us? How much worse does this get?"

"Being a loyal employee, and also new here, I kept my mouth shut until I could find out what happened that resulted in Shannon ending up down here. I hoped for a reasonable explanation, so I confronted Dickerson. First, he showed me the surveillance tapes he'd confiscated. One clearly showed me in a struggle with Shannon and later dragging him off the mall. Another showed Dickerson watching the scene from in front of his office. I doubt that tape exists now. He clearly explained that if I were to make waves, he would turn the tapes over to the authorities, and I would be arrested. If I kept my mouth shut the tapes would disappear. I knew how damning the tapes appeared, and my career, such as it is, would be over. It was too late to help Shannon, but I vowed to myself to find out what actually happened. And while at it to investigate the other recent deaths."

"What about Jerry, the night duty manager? He was present at the scene, late, but certainly a part of it. Didn't he investigate?"

"Probably, but Jerry was fired the next day, I was told."

"Oh, no. I hope his body doesn't turn up when the investigation begins. What was Dickerson's explanation for how Shannon ended up here?"

"He told me Shannon undoubtedly had a heart attack and died after escaping again that night, crawling down the side of the cliff and hiding in The Grotto. Now, I know for certain that he lied. The autopsy report has not been available for me to verify. I found out later from Samuel, the night guard, that he'd seen Dickerson give Shannon an injection of something after I left. Samuel guessed it was an antibiotic or a sedative. Now, I believe that it was lethal, whatever he used. I can't be certain yet, but the damage to the skin on his face and hands most likely resulted from Dickerson's dragging Shannon's body by the feet from the lab to the cave down here."

"Was Shannon such a threat to others?"

"Samuel told me that Dickerson and Sheila have been having an affair for several years. That would make it quite convenient to have Shannon under lock and key, and no doubt more convenient to have him dead."

"Oh, my God. What else can happen?"

"I believe he planned to kill both your mother and you."

"Why?"

"He knew I was bringing you two down here for the picnic. Garrick and Geoff had departed. Dickerson knew your mother's history with Burian sightings and that she'd spotted him when we were here before. I think he planned to lure you both to his cave and dispose of you. I also believe that all the fine furnishings in the staff quarters have been stowed with us after patients have been murdered—or even died naturally—and the families not notified while the trust funds continued to send monthly checks. You'll recall that I suggested this likelihood earlier, but then I hadn't tied the idea to killings, only natural deaths. It seems likely, too, that Dickerson was pocketing cash from sales of valuables and artifacts over time. We staffers were merely temporary custodians. Other than Sheila, few of us have had long enough tenure to recognize what was going on."

"Do you think she was in on his scam—and the murders?"

"No, I don't, after her confession of fear brought on by his strange behavior. I think she was guilty of infidelity, but without knowledge of murder and thievery. Time will tell, once the investigation and an audit begins. Had the holding company in London conducted audits prior to this, we might well have avoided such tragic consequences."

Lauren breathed deeply, trying to remain calm. "And where do you fit into this scenario?"

"Dickerson no doubt believed he had me over a barrel by blackmailing me and probably planning to eventually kill me, too. He was wrong. I would never have submitted to his blackmail. Temporarily, yes, but I was already making my own plans for exposing him. I just didn't know the extent of his evil." Kyle stopped, searched Lauren's eyes. "I hope you trust me. I am telling you the truth."

"I have to believe you, Kyle. You saved our lives today. I guess I don't understand how all this came to a head so suddenly."

"It probably wasn't as sudden as it seems. Sheila confided to me the day you arrived that she thought Dickerson was losing his mind. He'd been acting strange, detached from what was going on around him. She said he roughed her up pretty good a few nights earlier. She got away from him, but she's been afraid to be alone with him since then. She said she's applied on the QT for a new job off the island."

"Did she say what he did to her?"

"He tied her up and started babbling incoherently, apparently like he was doing tonight. She managed to work herself free and scrammed. She said she'd never seen him behave like that in the past."

"Then you think his mental deterioration was gradual but something triggered a break?"

"We may never know. He'd become more and more controlling over the past year, Sheila told me, more than a little unreasonable at times but not downright weird."

"I thought he was merely a sonofabitch," Lauren said.

"He was all of that, but you didn't see the strange looks he gave the staff at times. Almost spooky. I heard this from other techs. Since I'm a latecomer, I only noticed a time or two and attributed it to stress—or possibly an eye affliction. I'm surprised, however, that Sheila didn't pick up on it sooner."

"I still have a question. If you were on the mall in the middle of that night, how is it that you were on the shuttle with me coming from George Town the next day in the early afternoon?"

"Simple. Dickerson sent me by the early shuttle on one of his little drug missions, to get me out of the way while he fired Jerry, I believe now."

"You couldn't have had much sleep that night, but you didn't show it."

"I was too wired up to notice, plus I thought I was performing a good deed."

Three young men arrived with two stretchers. Kyle told them briefly what had happened, warning them not to remove Dickerson's body or touch anything inside the cavern until the authorities arrived. "The forensics people are on the way by helicopter and will need to take to take samples and photographs to thoroughly examine the scene. Nobody knows how many crimes have been committed here."

Fearful that wave action during high tide could wash away evidence near the entry to The Grotto before testing was accomplished, Kyle enlisted the men's help. Among them, they located and rolled, dragged or pushed several large boulders to block the opening.

As Kyle carried Mara from The Grotto, she began to wave her arms and legs. Her eyes fluttered open. "Is the picnic over?"

"Yes, Mom, it's over." Lauren thought maybe being out of touch with reality was not always such a bad thing.

Chapter

THIRTY

Mara and Lauren were taken to the infirmary for examination, Mara on a stretcher, at Kyle's insistence. He accompanied the group but assured everyone he was okay.

"I need to get over to the office to call the George Town authorities with fuller details. We need maximum help, and I only gave them bare facts."

Before he departed, he took Lauren aside to tell her Samuel had caught up with him as he emerged from the cliffside trail. Samuel revealed that he had recently discovered another opening to The Grotto, a shortcut from Dickerson's living quarters. When he'd asked Dickerson about it, the man had denied any knowledge that it existed. He forbade Samuel from exploring further or talking about it. He said he would see that the access was secured to prevent any nosy employees from being injured. "The route was, doubtless, the way Dickerson managed to drag Shannon's body there without help."

"But with great difficulty, considering the damage to the man by the time we found him." Lauren said. "Sadly, no one cared enough about Shannon to wonder where he might be."

"True."

After Mara regained full consciousness and her vital signs thoroughly checked, the women were released from the infirmary. Lauren guided her mother to Kyle's cottage against Mara's protests that she wanted to go to the dining room for an ice cream sundae.

As they approached the cottage, Lauren stopped, stunned to see Garrick and Geoff loom up before them. "I don't believe my eyes," she cried. "Am I hallucinating?"

"No," Geoff laughed. "We reached George Town but didn't feel good about leaving you two over here by yourselves."

Lauren laughed, at first mildly, then working into near-hysteria. "We weren't alone, were we, Mom?"

"I don't think so, but I believe I slept a lot."

"That's a fact," Lauren said. "But tell, me, gentlemen, what did you expect would happen to us?"

"No telling," Garrick growled. "In this environment, most anything, and you two women were unprotected. I didn't like your having to rely on that man."

"Well, 'that man' saved our lives and was otherwise most helpful. You won't believe what I have to tell you." She looked over at Garrick. "Or maybe you will."

They continued walking to Kyle's cottage where Lauren sat them down and proceeded to explain the bizarre events. The men stared in open-mouthed disbelief. When she reached the part about Mara and Garrick being correct in their identification of Kyle as the supposed killer, Garrick whooped.

"I knew I wasn't crazy. Hallelujah!"

Geoff looked a little skeptical. "At least he hasn't had any Phelan sightings in the past couple of days."

Mara, who had been observing silently, beamed. "I tried to tell them, but they wouldn't listen. They thought we were stupid."

"Now, who's the stupid one?" Geoff offered. "Seriously, I'm relieved to hear the outcome. That Dickerson was a mean bastard." He turned to Mara and apologized for his language. "I wonder who they'll put in his place?"

Kyle entered as if on cue. "I can answer you that one. I'm the temporary chief until the parent company finds a new one. Or, if my credentials check out, I may end up with the job."

"Congratulations," Geoff said.

Garrick looked incredulous.

Lauren asked, with a mock pout, "Then I guess you won't be going to New York?"

"No, but I can guarantee you it will be safe to leave your mother here. And Garrick, since I'm not the monster you presumed me to be, perhaps you'd like to stay as well. I could find some work for you interacting with the other … residents … on a voluntary basis, of course. You've been very helpful with Mrs. Edwards. Don't you agree, Lauren?"

"Yes, indeed. And I would be happy if Mother were to share his companionship for a long time. It's meant a great deal to both of us. What do you think, Geoff?"

"I think it's a helluva solution for everyone. Dad?"

Garrick hesitated, obviously thinking over the offer and the alternatives. "You don't know how long you'll be in charge," he directed at Kyle. From Garrick's expression, everyone present could see that he had not yet converted to believing in a good Kyle, a Kyle who would be their leader and friend.

"Right, I don't know how long I'll be here, but these things take time, so it could be six months or longer before I would be replaced. Then too, my credentials are quite good, so I think my chances are excellent. At any rate, it would give you more time to make up your minds about future arrangements."

"And what would you have me do with these other residents?" Garrick asked.

"You could very well teach writing classes as part of the occupational therapy program. Maybe even find your monthly charges reduced, and I'll be happy to look into that possibility. I just can't promise it yet."

A big smile split Garrick's face. "Geoff, I think he sold me."

Geoff looked relieved. "Think about it this way, Phelan and Burian will have new audiences."

Kyle laughed. "No telling what amazing creative works we'll add to the literary canon from Encantadora Island."

Lauren shuddered at the thought, then spoke up. "And I'll be going to New York by myself." She wouldn't have believed when she arrived that she could miss anyone here, other than her mother, but now she felt ties to these good folks who had been through such horror with her.

Kyle put his arm around her shoulders. "The best part, for me at least, is that you'll be back to visit your mom. You might even take longer vacations and bring your work here."

"I'll think about it. And, Geoff, will you still visit me in New York?"

"You can bet on it."

Garrick held out his hand to Kyle. "I owe you an apology, young man."

Kyle smiled with relief, grabbing Garrick's big paw with both hands to give it a hearty shake. "We need you here, man."

Mara beamed. "I'm happy when my children all get along."

My thanks go to two good friends, both published authors, who edited and proofread, tirelessly and with good-natured encouragement for this book reach print. Patricia Lutes and Lois Gentry your observations have been invaluable to me. Again, thank you.

CPSIA information can be obtained at www.ICGtesting.com
Printed in the USA
BVOW081921151112

305687BV00002B/7/P